INTRUDER
AT HAUNTED MESA

As Jenny stood gazing up at the deserted mesa, she thought she saw something move. She froze on the path, fixing her eyes upon the distant spot, trying to focus them clearly. Because what she saw didn't make a bit of sense. In fact, it couldn't be. What she seemed to be looking at was a giant with a blue head. Just for an instant she saw it, and then it was gone. But in that instant it had seemed to her like a very tall man with a large rectangle of blue for a head.

Yet surely there was nothing up there besides some rocks and a juniper bush or two. Had she mistaken a juniper bush?—but no, she knew she had not. She knew what she had seen. It was a giant with a blue head . . .!

SECRET
OF
HAUNTED MESA

Phyllis A. Whitney

A SIGNET BOOK
NEW AMERICAN LIBRARY
TIMES MIRROR

NAL BOOKS ARE ALSO AVAILABLE AT DISCOUNTS
IN BULK QUANTITY FOR INDUSTRIAL OR
SALES-PROMOTIONAL USE. FOR DETAILS WRITE TO
PREMIUM MARKETING DIVISION, NEW AMERICAN LIBRARY, INC.,
1301 AVENUE OF THE AMERICAS, NEW YORK, NEW YORK 10019.

COPYRIGHT © 1975 BY PHYLLIS A. WHITNEY

All rights reserved. No part of this book may be
reproduced in any form without permission in writing from
the publsher, except by a reviewer who wishes to quote
brief passages in connection with a
review in magazine or newspaper. For information address
The Westminster Press,
Witherspoon Building, Philadelphia, Pa. 19107.

Library of Congress Catalog Card Number: 75-4617

This is an authorized reprint of a
hardcover edition published by The Westminster Press.

SIGNET TRADEMARK REG. U.S. PAT. OFF. AND FOREIGN COUNTRIES
REGISTERED TRADEMARK—MARCA REGISTRADA
HECHO EN CHICAGO, U.S.A.

SIGNET, SIGNET CLASSICS, MENTOR, PLUME AND MERIDIAN BOOKS
are published by The New American Library, Inc.,
1301 Avenue of the Americas, New York, New York 10019

First Signet Printing, December, 1977

3 4 5 6 7 8 9

PRINTED IN THE UNITED STATES OF AMERICA

Contents

1. The Weeping Woman

The red heart of the campfire centered the night scene and made it pulse with a crimson glow. Juniper wood gave off a pungent scent that was pleasant on the air. Around the fire, logs and beams had been placed, offering seats for those who gathered near. The girl with flowing blond hair sat where firelight fell upon her lovely, uptilted face as she sang, her guitar resting on her knees. Circling the fire, the others sat quietly, watching the girl, listening to her music.

Farther away, the light faded into shadow, black near the trees, pale silver in the moonlight. Jenny Hanford sat on a flat rock well back from the others, almost lost in the surrounding shadows. She had no wish to be part of those listeners who hung so raptly upon her sister's singing. They were thrilled, of course, that the famous Carol Hanford was actually here in New Mexico at Haunted Mesa Ranch. Jenny was used to being in the background while everyone paid attention to Carol, but tonight she felt rebellious.

Her eyes searched the group to find her mother and father sitting close together, their attention focused as intently upon their elder daughter as though they had never before heard her sing. Jenny knew how troubled they were, how worried about Carol, yet tonight she couldn't sympathize. She couldn't help wishing they would sometimes look at her that way.

Deliberately she turned her attention from the scene and let her gaze wander over the great black mesa that rose behind the fire, its flat top like a ruled line against the starlit New Mexican sky. The scene was so beautiful it caught at her heart, even though she was tired of hearing Carol sing songs like "Rose of San Antone." Carol had shunned rock and given up on country music to specialize in old western songs—and it had certainly paid off for her. At fourteen she had become a prodigy. Television had been the perfect medium for what critics called her "intimate style," and she had been on most of the big shows. She had also done well at several festivals and her recordings had become enormously popular across the country. One was even a gold record. Now, at seventeen, her face and voice were known everywhere, and she loved nothing better than to take out her guitar and make a throng of listeners hang breathlessly on every sound she made.

Dad had tried to put his foot down—much too late. "This isn't all there is to life, Carol honey," he had said.

"For me it is," Carol had answered, and Jenny knew this was almost true for her beautiful and talented sister.

There! she was thinking about Carol again. And she didn't want to think about Carol. She had hoped that somehow, when her father had brought them all there this summer while he lectured on ecology for the Conference Center at Haunted Mesa Ranch, she would begin to be more of a person herself. She had had a vague notion that she might be able to make up a little for all that had gone wrong during this past year. It wasn't because she was dumb that she couldn't do her school work. She wasn't failing because she was stupid. It was just that she was no longer interested. She had stopped caring and that was a terrible feeling. But she was tired of teachers who said, "Oh, you're Carol Hanford's sister, aren't you? I remember her in eighth grade. She was so bright and pretty. We all loved her."

Okay, Jenny thought. *She* didn't have to be loved. *She* didn't want all that attention Carol thrived on. Or did she? Had she given up trying because it wasn't any use? How could anybody keep up with Carol Hanford? Dad and Mother had been disturbed about Jenny's nearly failing in school, but they seemed to think this was a passing thing. "What nonsense, Jenny," Dad had said. "You'll buckle down next term and do what is really very easy for you. You've always been a good student before." And he had gone back to arguing with Mother about Carol.

Carol didn't want to go to college. She wanted only to make a right-now career as a popular singer. She wanted to cut more records, sing with a group perhaps, play Vegas, and all the rest. The Hanfords had come out to the ranch this summer to get Carol away from all that for a while and try to make her see that she mustn't throw away her future. "There's all the time in the world ahead of you," Mother said.

"The singing will keep. Get to be a *person* first." So here they were—and there was Carol, singing as always.

Jenny clasped her hands about her knees and rocked back and forth, deliberately out of time with Carol, who had switched to "Red River Valley." They were all singing along with her now, but her strong, pure voice rose above the others.

"Ugh!" Jenny said to herself, expressing a great deal in the small, explosive sound.

She looked around the shadowy rim of the circle of listeners and for the first time noted that someone else shared the shadows with her. A little way off stood a tall woman with hair that was black and silver under the moon. Her sad, rather beautiful face was just touched by the firelight. She wore dark slacks and a light sweater against the cool evening air, and her arms were folded across her body as though she clasped herself for comfort, just as Jenny had done.

Glad to be distracted from the scene around Carol, Jenny watched the woman, wondering. There was something a little strange about her hunched shoulders and the fixed way she stared at the group about the fire. Curious, Jenny left her rock and edged a little closer. Now she could see the shine of tears on the pale, beautiful face, and the inward twist of the shoulders as the woman tried to control her sobbing.

Belatedly Jenny realized that this was something she should not be watching. This was deep, naked grief. There seemed hardly any reason to weep over Carol's singing of "Springtime in the Rockies," but that's what the woman was doing. Jenny took a backward step, meaning to lose herself in tree shadow before the woman saw that she had been observed, but her foot struck a stone that skittered and at once the weeping figure straightened and looked around.

She seemed to draw herself proudly erect as her eyes met Jenny's—great dark eyes that regarded her with displeasure. Then the woman turned away from the fire and walked off among the cottonwood trees, disappearing from view. Jenny was sorry. No one who was crying like that wanted to be watched, but she hadn't realized in time. She wondered who the woman was and why she had cried.

Restlessly she returned to her rock and sat down again. This singing bit could go on for hours. Now it was "On Top of Old Smoky." Sometimes Carol would sing alone, and sometimes she would encourage everyone to join in. There were several conferences being held at the Center, besides the ecology course her dad was lecturing for, and people from various groups had come together tonight to listen to Carol. There had been no hiding her under a bushel—not with that recognizable face. They had only been there two days when the woman who planned some of the social events for the Center had asked Mother if Carol would sing tonight. As if anybody could stop her!

Once more Jenny let her gaze wander off above the campfire so that the massive backdrop of the mesa filled her sight. She had never been west of the Mississippi before, and she had never seen a mountain like this. In the daylight its great rock mass was streaked with color—mostly red—and it was so close that it looked enormous. It stood up alone from the lower land, as other mesas did in the area, but where most of them were dotted with juniper, Haunted Mesa was sheer sandstone, with precipitous rock sides and only a few junipers clinging to the top. Someone had said those cliffs up there had been weathered and carved by a hundred million years of wind and storm.

She would like to climb up there to the very summit—if there was a way—where she would be able to see out over all the New Mexico countryside. But she had already heard the rule that was set down for everyone who came to the ranch. There were to be no long hikes, and no climbing without a suitable guide along. Sandstone was treacherous and it could crumble under your feet unless you knew where to walk.

Nevertheless she would love to be up there—away from Carol, away from the world. Jenny fixed her eyes on the line where the flat mesa top seemed to meet the sky and the stars that seemed so close above, and tried to shut out the sound of singing. Then something up there caught her attention. Surely something had moved along the mesa's rim. Against the lighter sky, a small black shape that she had taken for a juniper shrub had moved along the mesa's edge to another spot—and then was gone. Had she really seen it? Was there some animal up there? Surely it had not been a human figure on that great island of a mountain at night. Anyway, she couldn't find the shape or figure or whatever it was, and she gave up straining her vision on that high place. Lower movement had caught her attention now.

Someone near the edge of the fire had risen—or at least partly risen—stooping over so as not to be too much noticed, and was moving out of the circle of listeners, crawling almost on hands and knees. When the figure reached the outer edge it rose and she saw that it was a boy. He was coming in her direction and she waited with interest to see if he would notice her. It would be nice to have someone young to talk to at the ranch. So far she had seen very few young people here. The summer conferences were all for grown-ups.

Not only had he seen her, but he must have seen her before he left the fire because he was coming toward her deliberately.

"Hi," he said when he was close enough and she could make him out more clearly. There was enough light from the fire for her to tell that he must be about her own age and had brown hair and eyes, just as she did. Her own hair was long, in two braids down her back, and this boy wore his hair a little long, but neatly and curling in at the nape of his neck.

"Hi," she said in return, and waited. She had learned not to give out too much information too soon. Otherwise she'd start all that business of how-wonderful-that-you're-Carol-Hanford's-sister.

"I couldn't take any more of that close up," he said, and flung himself down on the ground beside her.

She liked him immediately. "Don't you enjoy singing?"

"Sure. I like rock. But I don't go much for country

and western. All those soppy old songs. You here with your parents?"

She nodded. He would have to work to get the Hanford name out of her, even if he wasn't enraptured by Carol.

"So'm I. Dad's here to take the ecology course that Carol's father is teaching."

"Oh?" Jenny said.

He raised himself on one elbow and stared at her in the flickering light. "You don't talk much, do you? My name's Greg Frost. What's yours?"

Well, it always happened. She couldn't hold out. "I'm Jenny Hanford."

He stared a little harder. "You mean you're *her* sister?"

Jenny nodded regretfully.

"Hey—I didn't mean to say anything to put her down. I expect she's—"

"You can say anything you want," Jenny broke in, and heard the edge to her own voice.

Greg sat up cross-legged and seemed to consider this. "Yeah," he said after a while. "I know. I've got two older brothers. I'm just as glad they're having a summer in Scandinavia this year."

"You have?" Jenny was interested and a little more hopeful. "What are they like?"

"Oh, they aren't like Carol over there, but they can do all sorts of things I can't do and they waste a lot of time trying to put me down. I don't put down so easy."

Jenny smiled at him. "No, I guess you don't. Carol doesn't try to put me down. She's sort of fond of me, I suppose. It's just that—"

"Don't tell me, let me guess." He put on a prim look and nodded at her, but she could see the mischief dancing in his eyes. "Oh, so you're Carol Hanford's little sister? How *won*derful! Do you think you could get her autograph for me?"

Jenny's smile turned into a chuckle and she doubled over. This boy was the best thing that had happened in her life for a long time. He was about the first person she had ever met who understood. She tried out the game herself.

"And so you're the little brother of those wonderful boys I had in my eighth-grade class? Though of course I can't expect *you* to turn out so well. You don't look—I mean—oh, of course—"

Greg was not the sort who laughed quietly. He roared his laughter so loudly that Jenny saw some of the people on their side of the campfire look toward them, and even Carol turned her head.

"Ssh!" Jenny whispered, and Greg subsided.

"I'm glad I found you," he whispered back. "There don't seem to be any other kids around this place. Maybe we can stir things up a little while we're here."

"Stir things up?"

"Sure. Don't you like to have people pay attention to you some of the time, instead of to her?"

"Well, yes. I suppose so. But I don't see how. Nothing takes Mother's and Dad's attention away from Carol these days. Not even my nearly failing in school."

"Failing? Is that what you tried?"

Her eyes widened as she stared at him. What did he mean? Was that why she had nearly failed? Because she thought they would be concerned and fuss over her, even if it was only to scold her? She hadn't really thought of it like that, and the idea made her uncomfortable.

"Kidding yourself, weren't you?" Greg said.

She couldn't accept that and shook her head indignantly. "It's just that I got so bored. Nothing exciting ever happens to me, and school didn't seem to matter anymore."

"There are ways to make things happen. Ways that are more fun than to get bad marks in school."

"For instance?"

Mischief was alight in his eyes again and his grin was engaging. She didn't think there was any real harm in Greg Frost, but she also sensed that he might cause waves wherever he was. Rather big ones, and she wasn't sure she could swim in that kind of rough sea.

"Believe me," he said, "nobody pays much attention to my brothers when I'm around."

"But what can I do? Maybe Carol is taking up all my mother's and father's time right now because it's necessary. Maybe that's how it has to be until things get straightened out a little."

"Is that how you want it to be?"

"No, I guess not." She sighed, and there was unhappiness in the sound.

"Hey!" Greg reached out and patted her shoulder. "Don't let it get to you. Try something."

"What?"

"You have to figure that one out. I can't do it for you. But do something—unexpected. Break a rule.

Get in trouble. Just a little trouble—so they have to rescue you. Get a few people excited."

Jenny sighed again. "I can't think of anything." She looked once more at the top of the great mountain that overhung the scene. "I suppose I could climb up there."

"No." He shook his head vehemently. "The climb up there is supposed to be easy if you know the way. If you don't, it's dangerous. So don't do anything silly where you could get hurt. That'll bring you attention you don't want. But you'll think of something. You'll get an idea."

Her look still rested on the faraway top of the mesa. She changed the subject. "Were you looking up there a while ago? Did you see anything move on top?"

He stared up at the great mountain. "No, of course not. There's nothing up there. I was reading about it. There are just some old Indian ruins on top. But the only time anybody goes up there now is when a group from the ranch is taken on a hike to the top."

"Why do they call it Haunted Mesa?"

"I don't know exactly. I think some people died up there."

She let the matter go and stood up, stretching. People around the campfire were applauding. Carol had stopped singing and was putting her guitar aside. The group was breaking up, some of them moving out of the circle.

"Guess I'll go look for my dad and mom," Greg said. "See you tomorrow." And he was gone before she had found anything she could say to thank him for cheering her up. His presence at the Center made things seem a little brighter—and he certainly had given her something to think about. Not that she was sure his advice was very good. In some ways he was a strange boy, with rather a big chip on his shoulder.

She started along the dirt road leading down the hillside to the family cottages that rayed out from the lodge and the conference buildings. Unlike Greg, she had no wish to find her parents and walk back to the cottage with them and a keyed-up Carol. She would have to listen to Carol long enough after she had gone to bed. Not that her sister could help what happened to her. After she had been singing— even informally like this—and there had been applause and admiration, she got terribly wide awake and stirred up and excited. She wanted to talk over every detail of her performance, and she never understood that a younger sister might be pretty bored with the whole thing.

So Jenny ambled along by herself, following the curving road that ran down the hill. She had several things to think about and she wanted to be alone and uninterrupted for as long as possible. It wasn't dark on the road because there were lights ahead around the Conference Center and in the windows of the dormitory building. From the porch ceiling of every cottage hung a lighted lantern.

As she followed the road she found herself passing the one place that was forbidden to those visiting the ranch. A low adobe wall surrounded a one-story adobe house. Since she had seen the house in the daytime, she knew that a turquoise trim had been painted around the windows, and the gate was turquoise blue. Now the curtains were drawn across the windows, and there were lights behind them indicating that someone lived there. This was private property, as the conference notices had warned, and no one must disturb the owner.

As she went by, Jenny looked over the wall and in the light cast from a window she could see a neat strip of garden, in itself unusual for this area where there was little rain and few gardens. The house looked somehow warm and inviting, and Jenny wondered who lived there in such seclusion and didn't want to be bothered with visitors.

But she had her own affairs to think about and she went on past other cottages, heading for Juniper. Adobe, or a combination of adobe and cement, had been used throughout the grounds, so there was a Spanish-Indian look about all the cottages. Each one had a name—Piñon, Cottonwood, Aspen, Tamarack, and so on. Their own cottage had the name Juniper on a sign over the door, and the light that hung from the ceiling of the small porch was housed in an iron lantern.

Jenny paused for one more look at the high mesa standing alone and massive in the moonlight. Though she stared for a moment, nothing moved up there, and she went up the low steps and into the Hanford cottage. It wasn't very large, but it had two neatly furnished bedrooms, with a bath between. Dad and Mother shared one room, and Carol and Jenny the other. She touched the switch at the door and the shaded overhead light came on.

A rag rug on the floor made the room look cheerful, and the furniture was bright maple, of simple construction. A reading lamp stood on the table between the twin beds, and a book lay on Jenny's pillow beside a small wooden carving she had placed there.

But she did not feel like reading now. She wanted to think quietly in these few moments when she could still be alone. Carol would be one of the last to leave the campfire, because people would hang around talking to her, staring at her. Funny, how they stared—as though she couldn't be real, just because they had seen her on television or as though they expected her to have two heads. The grown-ups weren't any better than the kids.

Jenny smiled to herself as she picked up the small wooden figure from her pillow and sat down in the room's one chair, turning the carving about in her fingers. On the drive to Haunted Mesa Ranch, north from Santa Fe, they had stopped at a village where there were wood-carvers. Jenny had been fascinated by all the carvings of desert creatures displayed on the shelf of one small shop, and she had fallen so in love with this humorous carving of a roadrunner that she had bought it with her own money.

This was her lucky piece, she told herself as she sat in the cottage chair, once more admiring the silly-looking bird with its huge tail, long beak, and earnest expression. It was poised on the block of wood as though it were running. On the bottom of the decorated block was the penciled name "Alice," and Jenny wondered about the Alice who had so lovingly carved this amusing little fellow.

Nevertheless, she knew that what she was doing

was only a delaying tactic. Sooner or later she had to face up to what Greg had said and really think about it. "Do something unexpected," he had told her. "Get in a little trouble." "Get people excited." She wasn't sure she would enjoy any of that. She didn't especially like to upset people or make them angry. Yet the fact remained that she was awfully, awfully tired of being Carol's shadow, and a little risk might be worth it, if only to switch her mother's and father's attention seriously to her for a while.

"Do you think I could do it?" she asked the roadrunner.

His tiny, indented eyes looked at her perkily out of the wood as though he were saying, "Go ahead!"

A sort of tingle went through her as a sudden idea popped into her mind. Something that might be possible. And it wasn't anything very bad. Yet it might work.

Down the path from the cottage she could hear Carol's unmistakable voice, kindled with excitement, while Mother's lower tones tried to quiet and calm her. In a sudden rush Jenny tore off her clothes, pulled on her pajamas, and dived into bed, drawing the covers up to her ears, pretending to be asleep.

It didn't do any good. When Carol came in, she wanted as always to talk and Jenny had to listen. But at the back of her mind the idea was growing, taking shape. Tomorrow—perhaps tomorrow.

2. The Giant
with a Blue Head

Breakfast was rather fun. All meals were cafeteria style, and the big dining hall was bright and airy with windows all around, and the sun wasn't hot yet. Since Jenny's father was a lecturer at a conference, the family had their own small table instead of sitting at the long tables with the conference members. Jenny saw Greg across the room and he waved to her, but she had no chance to talk to him again.

Carol had not come to breakfast. She always slept late after keeping herself awake half the night, and she knew Mother would bring her something from breakfast to eat later. But Dad had an early class, and Mother liked to be with him at meals and so did Jenny.

Somehow Jenny did not feel so gloomy that morning. Greg had cheered her up. She was not quite so alone with her problems as she had been before. It helped to know that someone else had problems of the same kind. And the notion that had come to her last night kept up a sort of tingling in her mind—as if it were demanding attention. She put it off comfortably. It was enough to have it there if things became desperate and she decided to try Greg's plan.

She glanced around the room at groups chattering at other tables, and then looked back at her father and mother. She was frequently glad they weren't fat, and that Mother was nice-looking, with dark brown hair that she wore in curly bangs over her forehead and pinned into a soft pile at the back of her head. Dad was tall, a little gray above the ears, and very earnest-looking. He enjoyed talking about serious matters and often held long discussions with close friends on scientific or political subjects, and Mother often joined in. But this morning neither parent looked cheerful, and their discussion was entirely about Carol.

"It's too bad this had to happen so soon," Mother said. "If only no one had caught on to who she is right away. Now she's off on that pink cloud again, with everyone adoring her."

"I never could understand why anyone would want to be adored by a lot of strangers she'll never see again," Dad said.

Jenny thought of Greg and his mischief, and put a passing thought into words, surprising herself considerably: "*I* would like to be adored by anybody at all," she announced.

Mother choked on her coffee. Dad put his fork down and stared at her.

"That's an idiotic notion," he said. "One in the family is enough."

But Mother laughed, a bit ruefully, and put out a hand to cover Jenny's on the table. "We aren't really neglecting you, darling. It's just that Carol is facing a decision that will affect her whole life, and we've got to figure out how to convince her of something she doesn't want to do."

In the meantime, Jenny thought, *my* life is *now*—and I'm just a big zero that nobody ever worries about or pays any attention to. It wasn't just a momentary thing, as Mother had implied. If they weren't rushing off to get Carol to some studio on time, they were answering phones, making appointments, dealing with reporters. Dad got out of a lot of that since he was away most of the day teaching in a Long Island college. But it went on and on for Mother.

Anyway, just for a moment Greg's idea had worked. She had spoken up unexpectedly, and her parents had both looked at her and forgotten Carol for about all of one minute.

After breakfast Mother had some letters to write, and she wanted to stay around until Carol got up. Dad had his early class, so Jenny could do as she liked. She took out the printed map that had been given to conference members and studied it. She had already been down to the corral block to watch the horses and burros. She hadn't gone to the museum at Haunted Mesa Ranch yet, although it was supposed to be a fine one of things Southwestern. But she postponed that for now. Another place appealed to her more at the moment. She had not yet visited the far corner of the property where a small square on the map noted the first house that had been built on Haunted Mesa Ranch. *Where original owners lived*, the notation at the bottom of the map said.

Carol stirred in bed and blinked sleepily as Jenny rustled the map.

"Hi, Jenny-Penny," she said, sounding half awake, but cheerful.

Carol always woke up in a good humor. In fact, she had a good disposition most of the time—unless someone tried to keep her from being a famous singer. Now she raised herself on one elbow and yawned widely.

"Wasn't it heavenly last night?" Carol went on.

This was not something that required an answer, so Jenny was silent, busying herself with making her bed.

"Tell you what," Carol went on. "After I've waked up enough and found something to eat, maybe we can get a couple of burros and go for a ride."

"Mm," Jenny said, not turning around. She knew what any sort of expedition with Carol would be like. They would start out fine, but before long people would appear from nowhere. The boy who saddled the burros, the ranch hands, everybody would stand around and stare sheepishly, while Carol smiled at them all and talked to them graciously. By the time she and Jenny started off, there would be additional riders in the party. Carol would be surrounded and happily the center of attention. Jenny would straggle along at the tail end of the party and no one would even speak to her. Except Carol. After a while Carol would look around and send somebody to fetch her. Then they would all notice Jenny too—because Carol included her and after all she was Carol Hanford's sister.

"I—I've got other things to do," Jenny said. She set the little roadrunner back on her pillow and went to tell her mother she was going to go down and look at the place where the original owners had lived. On the way she would keep an eye open for Greg. He might have some ideas on how to spend the morning.

The sun was higher now as she stepped onto the little porch and looked out over the tremendous sweep of land that was visible from the ranch. The Conference Center was built on a rise of hill below Haunted Mesa, and you could look out over empty, juniper-spotted land to distant mountains. Over on the right rose the strange configuration of Finger Rocks that spiked up from a sandstone ridge, and there were other, smaller mesas too. The colors of the land and the rocks were fascinating—dun and yellow and red, with green polka dots of the stubby junipers everywhere. In some places junipers grew to be tall trees, but in this part of the country they were all stunted. In fact, trees were rare, and mostly they were cottonwoods or piñon pines.

A sound nearby caught her attention and she stepped down from the porch and looked around. There was another cottage—Aspen—next door, but no one seemed to be near it. Nevertheless, she had the curious feeling that someone had been watching her. It made her a little uncomfortable, but since everything around seemed quiet in the warming sunshine, she shrugged off the impression and started downhill in the direction the map had indicated. Most of the cottages had emptied for classes, but here and there someone waved to her and even as she waved back, she couldn't help wondering if they were being friendly because she was Carol's sister.

In a little while she had left the cluster of conference buildings and cottages behind. The dirt road narrowed to a path, and the dry reddish earth sent little spurts of powdery dust into the air as she put her feet down. The sky seemed enormous overhead, without a cloud in sight, and the air was sparkling clean and invigorating to breathe. Mother had had a little trouble in Santa Fe, tiring quickly and getting out of breath because she wasn't used to the altitude, but Jenny didn't mind it.

A stand of cottonwood trees closed in behind her, and for a short distance she could walk in shade. When she was in the open again, she could see the small wooden shack ahead that was the oldest landmark at Haunted Mesa Ranch. The windows had been boarded up but the door had not been locked and it creaked on its hinges as she pulled it open. A bit doubtfully she peered inside. Sunlight poured in the door behind her, lighting the bare interior, and after a moment of listening she stepped across the splintery threshold.

There was no furniture left, except for a three-legged table shoved against one wall. An echoing emptiness inside the shack seemed to follow her as she moved around, and in a way it was reassuring. No one was here but Jenny Hanford. The tiny place appealed to her. She always liked the feeling of being alone, of exploring something all by herself where no intruders could distract her with their notions and ideas or tell her what to do and what to think.

On the far wall of the tiny main room hung a faded calendar with an old-fashioned picture of an

Indian girl in fringed buckskin, wearing a beaded band around her head. Beneath the picture was a caption that read: *A Maiden of the Plains.* But the Plains Indians didn't come from around here, and from what she had read about Pueblo Indians, Jenny knew they had never dressed like that. She had a picture at home of a Pueblo woman of the old days in a roughly woven dress, with one shoulder bare. She wore white leggings and the kind of moccasins that were known as "squaw boots" on her feet. Anyway, the younger Indians that Jenny had seen in Santa Fe dressed like everyone else. The older ones who sat under the long portal before the Governor's Palace on the plaza had worn blankets around their shoulders in the cool of the morning. They were selling turquoise jewelry and other small craftwork laid out on mats on the sidewalk before them, and Mother had bought Carol and Jenny each a silver-and-turquoise bracelet with a thunderbird design.

But it was not the Indian girl's picture that interested her most. The month that hung exposed read "September, 1935." More than forty years ago. Was that the last date that the owners of the ranch had lived in this place? Who were they and why had they moved away? If they were owners, they must not have been poor. Why would they live in a rickety little house like this?

Forty years was an enormously long time. Her parents had been babies then.

She moved on to a small adjoining room that must have been a bedroom. Here, with the one window boarded over, it was dim and dusty. She could smell the old dust as it stirred beneath her feet. Another door opened on to a small kitchen with a rusty sink, its enamel badly chipped. Over the sink hung a cracked mirror and Jenny looked at her own wide-eyed face in the shadowy glass, shivering pleasantly. It was as if she were a ghost coming back to visit the abandoned place, looking hazily out of the crazed mirror.

The door of the kitchen stood partly ajar as she had left it, and she noticed something hanging on a hook behind it. Some article of clothing it seemed to be. How strange that something should have been left hanging here all those years. Curious now, she reached up and took it down, sneezing as dust rose from the grubby folds. When she held the thing up in the shadowy light she could see that it was a faded yellow smock—a woman's smock, judging by its size, with long sleeves on which there were smears of paint.

An artist's smock? But why? Why here? Why hadn't it been taken away when the owners left this place—why had it been left here all these years? Not that it was worth anything. She saw that there was paint on the front of it too, and a pocket was torn loose. She felt in each pocket. The torn one was empty, but in the other was a small round object which she drew out.

It was a tarnished Indian head penny. How very strange.

She loved the strangeness. It was full of mystery. Long after Dad's conference was over, she would remember the adventure of finding this place. Most people would have little interest in a ramshackle house like this. Probably, year after year, no one disturbed it. And that made another mystery. Why hadn't it been torn down? Nothing else on the ranch was dilapidated. Jenny Hanford had walked across these floors, and in a sense brought the house to life. When she left she would take something of this place with her in her imagination. She would think of it as a secret with a story of its own. And because she didn't know the real story, she would make up tales about the people who had lived here, and especially about the woman who had worn the yellow smock and left a penny in its pocket when she went away, with only that calendar on the wall to tell when she had gone.

Carefully, Jenny hung the ragged garment back on its hook, because that was where it lived, restored the penny to the pocket where she had found it, and returned to what must have been the bedroom. And as she stood there studying the wreaths of cobwebs in the corners and draped down the walls, she heard a sound that startled her in the lonely place.

That rusty creaking could mean only one thing. Someone had pulled wide the front door she had left half open—someone who was even now stepping into the shack's main room. Instinctively, Jenny moved behind the bedroom door. She didn't know why she was suddenly frightened—except that it was very lonely there, and out of call of the rest of the conference grounds. And she still remembered that odd, out-of-place movement on top of the mesa last night, as though someone had been up there, regardless of what Greg had said. Someone who, perhaps, shouldn't have been there. Someone who watched.

Footsteps crossed the bare boards of the floor and a voice called out, echoing through the shack. "Hey, Jenny! Are you here, Jenny?"

She laughed in relief as the tension flowed out of her. It was only Greg, and she went into the other room to greet him. Greg was the one person who might understand her feelings about this deserted place.

"You scared me for a minute when I heard the door creak," she admitted. "I didn't know anyone was around."

"I saw you heading this way and I thought I'd follow you. Our cottage is right next to yours."

This was a pleasant surprise. "I heard someone around that cottage this morning. I had a feeling someone was watching me. Was it you?"

He shook his head. "No. I was over in the dining hall. We got there just before it closed. When I came out I saw you going by, so I came along."

Uneasily, Jenny wondered who could have been watching from behind the next cottage, but put the thought quickly aside. There was too much to tell Greg now.

She showed him the calendar with its long-ago date and led him into the other rooms, let him see the yellow smock hanging on the back of the kitchen door. She even took out the tarnished Indian head penny and held it out to him.

"It's all so strange, isn't it?" she said. "I wonder what the woman was like who wore this smock?"

Greg looked at the date on the penny and gave it back to her to return to the pocket. "You can see her anytime you want," he said.

She stared at him. "What do you mean?"

"You know that big adobe house that everyone is warned to stay away from? That's where she lives. I've heard about her. Her husband put up this little shack for them to live in while the adobe house was being built. She's Spanish American, from Santa Fe, but she married an Anglo—Paul Eliot—so her name is Consuelo Valdez Eliot."

"Paul Eliot," Jenny repeated. "I think I've heard that name somewhere."

"Probably. If you've read anything about Indians of the Southwest, you may have read some of his books. My dad says he was one of the best writers about Indians."

"Was?"

"Yes. He died about six months ago. So now Señora Consuelo—that's what they call her around here—lives in that adobe house alone."

"I wonder if she's an artist?" Jenny said.

"I wouldn't know. Anyway, the ranch got to be too much for the Eliots to keep up and they made a gift of it to a New Mexico university to use for conferences. They haven't owned the ranch for years, but there was an arrangement, when they made the gift, for the Eliots to live in their house for the rest of their lives. And no one can tear down this shack. Now that Mrs. Eliot's left alone, she doesn't want to see anybody from outside or talk to anyone but her old friends. I heard it didn't use to be that way. It's just since her husband died. But that's why everyone is warned not to bother her or trespass on her private grounds."

Jenny had hardly thought again of the woman she had seen weeping in the shadows the night before, but now she remembered her.

"I think I've seen her. I think she came to listen to Carol's singing last night."

But Greg had lost interest in Mrs. Eliot—Señora Consuelo. "How are you doing on that plan to stir things up?" he asked.

That was one thing Jenny didn't want to talk about. The thought she had had last night didn't look quite so good this morning, and anyway it was too vague to be called a plan. If she tried it and it didn't work, she didn't want Greg to know. He would think she should have figured out something better. Besides, this information about Mrs. Eliot might make a difference. Even that yellow smock hanging on a hook in this shack might make a difference.

"I haven't thought of anything good yet," she said.

"Well, let's get out of this dusty old place. It gives me the creeps."

So he hadn't understood after all. He didn't feel about it the way she did. But she followed when he led the way outside.

"How about taking a hike up to the foot of Haunted Mesa?" he asked. "We won't go up, of course, but we could look for where the trail begins. It's not very far."

"Not now," she said. "Maybe another time."

At another time she might have been eager to follow his lead, but now she wanted to be alone again and not be pestered to come up with a "plan."

"If you just keep putting it off," Greg said, "you'll

never do anything. Nobody treats *me* like Little Brother anymore, and you must have a much worse situation to stop. They *will* stop, you know, if you make people pay attention to *you*."

"Mm," Jenny said, not committing herself. "I have to think about it for a while. I don't want to rush into anything silly."

He grinned at her, but he wasn't being as sympathetic as he had been last night. The mischief in his brown eyes seemed a little mocking.

"Aren't you still wishing something exciting would happen to you?" he asked.

"Something exciting is happening." Jenny nodded toward the little house behind her. "I'll always remember this."

"I meant something really exciting," Greg said. "Anyway, stay here and think about it if you want. I'm going to have a look at that trail up the mesa, because someday I'm going up there."

"Last night you said it was dangerous if you don't know the way."

"Sure. But I won't go alone. I'll find somebody to take me. If you're still around, maybe you can go too."

"I'd like that," she said sincerely, but when he waved his hand and started up the path that led back to the Conference Center, she did not follow him. The mesa would keep. She had a lot to think about and puzzle out.

The tall, slim figure of the woman standing where the campfire glow just touched her was very clear in her mind, and the figure had seized her imagination,

just as the little house had done. Jenny could
remember the hair swept softly back from the face,
with its blackness and its silver streaks. She could
remember the shine of tears on that truly beautiful
face, and she found her own throat tightening in
sympathy, because now she knew the tragedy behind
the tears. She didn't understand why the singing had
made the woman weep, but her sorrow seemed to
transfer itself to Jenny, so that she felt sad too,
remembering. Surely that had been Mrs. Eliot. She
was more real now because Jenny had stood in the
tiny house where she had lived with her husband
long ago when she was young. Perhaps when they
were first married. Forty years ago! More than that.
There was surely some meaning in that yellow
smock hanging on its hook with the penny in its
pocket.

Jenny's "plan"—Greg-inspired—had to do with that
adobe house that was out-of-bounds. But now that
she knew something about the woman who lived
there, she didn't think she could carry it through.

It wasn't a very good plan anyway. What if she did
go deliberately over that wall, or through the blue
gate—if it was open—nothing very startling would
happen. She had thought first in terms of an angry
owner reporting her to the conference director, of
his talking sternly to her mother and father to tell
them their younger daughter had broken the rules.
But that was silly. No one would bother about her to
that extent. Probably someone would just come to
tell her to go away, and nothing at all would result.
It would be pretty stupid if she went to her mother
and said she had climbed over into forbidden terri-

tory and someone had told her to leave. Her mother would just think she'd gone bananas to get excited about nothing—and she'd go right back to talking about Carol.

And yet . . . The adobe house was like a magnet that drew her. She really didn't need to trespass. She would just like to look at the house more carefully and think about the woman and the smock. Perhaps she would catch another glimpse of Mrs. Eliot—though without letting her know she was being watched.

Jenny stood up with new resolution. There was no harm in this changed plan, and it appealed to her. She turned back in the direction of the Center, which meant that she also turned toward Haunted Mesa. The mountain stood up with its great stark mass shining in the eastern sunlight of morning, its steep sides stained with red and streaks of purple. In different lights the colors changed and it was always fascinating to watch. Now at the very top, at the front rim of the mesa, overlooking the ranch below, something moved.

Jenny froze on the path, fixing her eyes upon that distant spot, trying to focus them clearly. Because what she saw didn't make a bit of sense. In fact, it couldn't be. What she seemed to be looking at was a giant with a blue head. Just for an instant she saw it, and then it was gone. But in that instant it had seemed to her like a very tall man with a large rectangle of blue for a head.

Now she wished Greg were here. She needed someone to check on her own vision. There were only rocks up there. And a juniper bush or two clinging to the jagged top. Had she mistaken a juniper bush?—but no, she knew she had not.

She knew what she had seen. It was a giant with a blue head.

3. Through the Turquoise Gate

Something was going on up on top of the mesa, Jenny thought, as she started along the path toward the Center. But if she told anyone what she had seen, she would simply be laughed at. And anyway, what did she know about this place after being here only a few days? It still seemed odd that someone might have been up there in the dark last night, but none of it was really her business and she had other things to think about.

The path seemed shorter going back, even though it was uphill, and in no time the conference buildings had come in sight. When the path widened to a dirt road, she chose the left-hand fork which would take her past the adobe house.

As she neared the house, she began to walk more slowly. If she hurried too much, she would be past it before she saw anything. Already she was opposite the low wall. It too was made of adobe and molded into a rounded top that came only as high as her shoulders. She would not go over it, of course, but she walked close beside it and looked beyond at the small strip of garden between wall and house that she had noticed last night. She realized now that it was like no other garden she had ever seen. There was no grass, and the earth was the same tawny sand color, a little reddish, that she had seen all around the ranch. Growing close to the house was an assortment of desert plants. There were low gray-green bushes, a tall plant with branching arms, and all sorts of spiny cactuses. Some were small and rounded, with prickles all over them. Others had joints growing one from another, branching in different directions.

She had never seen so many cactus plants before. When she reached the gate, painted to match the blue trim around the deep-set windows of the house, and found it ajar, she stopped to peer through the opening. Beyond the gate the house drowsed in morning sunshine. Its curtains were open, and through the window on the right of the front door she could glimpse a long, shadowy room. Then the door itself took her attention. It was a wooden door, large and intricately carved, and must have been made by hand. It stood wide open upon an entryway tiled in warm red.

There was no one about and her interest was growing. Of course if Mrs. Eliot appeared, she would just look at her quickly and then walk away fast. She wouldn't want her to think she was spying—especially after she had been caught staring last night. But the desert garden and the house itself fascinated her. She knew instinctively that it would be beautiful inside. It would be a house that would suit the woman with the beautiful face whom she had seen last night.

No one stirred anywhere, and the gate stood open.

Perhaps she could just step through it for a moment and look a little more closely. Then she would have that much more for her imagination to turn over when she got home. She would be able to think about the woman who had lived in the shack with the yellow smock on a hook, and the woman who lived in this lovely, unusual house. When she got home these things would be as real for her in her mind as the Hanfords' house and garden back on Long Island.

Three steps took her through the open gate, and now she could see the entryway more clearly, with its red tiles and a glowing picture of sunflowers on the wall. Everything was quiet, nothing moved. Of course if anyone appeared, she would turn like a coward and run through the gate, off in the direction of the Center. No one need ever know who she was. She had no desire now to get into the trouble that Greg had suggested. It was just that her own fascination with this place was not to be denied.

Then the one thing she hadn't thought of happened. Behind her someone came through the gate—and she was trapped. She whirled around, feeling guilty and apologetic, to face the plump figure of a Spanish-American woman with a basket in her hands. Her dark eyes snapped with indignation as she confronted Jenny, and she closed the gate rather sharply behind her.

"What are you doing here, little girl? Do you not know you must not come to this house? It is posted at the Center that no one is to disturb Señora Consuelo. You are bad to come here. I will report you! I will—"

A woman's calm voice spoke from the doorway of the house. "What is the matter, Maria?"

Maria waved an excited hand at Jenny. "It is this child from the Center! She has come through our gate! She is—"

Once more the calm, emotionless voice broke in. "Who are you?" it asked Jenny.

Jenny turned from Maria to face the woman who had come out to the red tile doorstep and stood with one hand resting against the great carved door. This morning she wore a long handwoven cotton robe that was almost the same deep rust-red as the mesa, and, while her face was still as beautiful as it had seemed by moonlight, Jenny could see the lines drawn between the brows and the crescents of age around the mouth. She didn't look angry, and her eyes were not disapproving as they had seemed the night before. She didn't look anything—neither angry nor sad nor anything else. Her face was like a mask—empty.

Somehow Jenny found her voice. "I—I'm Jenny Hanford," she said. "My father is teaching at the ecology conference."

"Then you're the sister of that girl who sings?"

Here it was again. It always happened. Jenny raised her head and met the dark eyes that looked at her without any real interest. Quite suddenly she decided that she didn't like Mrs. Eliot. She wasn't at all the person of her imagination. The real woman was spoiling all the things Jenny wanted to remember when she went away from Haunted Mesa. Abruptly she had had enough. Enough of all the years of being Carol's sister.

"I'm *me*," she told the woman. "What difference does it make whether Carol Hanford is my sister?"

Something flickered in the dark eyes. "Why did you come here? Why did you come through my gate when you must know that I've asked to have no visitors?"

Jenny did not let her eyes drop, and she no longer felt apologetic. "I came because of that yellow smock with the penny in its pocket," she said.

There was a slight cracking of the mask as surprise came into the woman's eyes. "Whatever do you mean?"

How could she answer that? It was bad enough that she had spoken those unexplainable words, but how could she tell this cold stranger what she had felt about that little shack with the ragged yellow smock hanging on a hook? She wasn't sure she herself understood what it was that had so seized her imagination, and she tightened her lips grimly, not attempting to speak. This time she let her gaze drop and stared at the reddish-tan dust at her feet.

Maria broke into words again. "I will send her away, Señora. I will tell to the director of the Center that this girl has come here. She will be punished, and we will have no more trouble."

Señora Consuelo paid no attention. She seemed to have removed herself to some distant place where she was lost in her own thoughts. After a moment she stepped aside from the doorway.

"Please come in," she said to Jenny. "I want you to tell me about the yellow smock with the penny in the pocket."

For an instant Jenny could not move. But the door

was open and the woman stood waiting. Feeling a little frightened now, Jenny obeyed the command of that waiting figure. Behind her, Maria spluttered a bit as she disappeared around the house. When she stepped onto those red tiles, Jenny Hanford was alone with Consuelo Eliot.

"To your right," Señora Consuelo said, and Jenny went through an arched adobe door into a long, cool room that at once appealed to all her senses. Oblong Indian rugs of red and white and gray covered the red tiles of the floor, simple and pleasing in their woven designs. The furniture seemed to be mainly brown and green, with touches of rust, and one wall was covered by books in colored jackets. Here and there were Indian ornaments—a basket of brown and white, a great pottery vase with hunting figures running about its plump sides. On the walls were paintings of New Mexican scenes—one of the cathedral in Santa Fe, one of an Indian pueblo with tiered rooms and ladders leading from one level to another. The fireplace too was of adobe and it occupied a corner of the room. On the wall nearby hung a long strand of dried chili peppers and a bunch of Indian corn, speckled with black and red and blue kernels. Next on the wall hung a handsome painting that was surely of Haunted Mesa itself.

Jenny spoke for the first time. "Did you paint that?" she asked, looking up at the mesa picture.

"I wish I had." The woman's voice was low and rather sad, but pleasing in its tone. "Why would you think so?"

"There was paint on the yellow smock," Jenny said.

Señora Consuelo seemed to puzzle over this. "When I left that smock on its hook I didn't know that I'd be revealing so much to someone who would come here forty years later."

"More than forty years in September," Jenny said. "I saw the calendar."

Something that was almost a smile touched the woman's lips. "Come and sit down, young Jenny. I used to paint. Not pictures. I used to make pottery. I learned from a Navaho friend. And it was pottery I painted. I made that big jar over there."

Jenny looked again at the jar with the brown decoration of Indian hunters, studying it in wonder. "It's very beautiful," she said as she sat down in a deep chair, once more looking all around the room. It didn't seem quite real to be sitting here in this house, talking to this woman. Jenny tilted her head and looked up at the ceiling in further satisfaction because the brown wooden beams that ran the length of the room, with the spaces between painted white, were exactly right for this house. She had seen ceilings like this in Santa Fe, with the same brown beams supporting adobe roofs. From outside, you could see the ends of the beams protruding from the roofs.

"Those beams are called vigas," the woman said. "It's a Spanish word."

Jenny repeated the sound. "Vigas. I wish all ceilings were made like that. I like them."

"They suit the Southwest. Where are you from, Jenny Hanford?"

"New York. A town on Long Island. I've never been in New Mexico before. I guess that's why I got so interested in looking at your house. At least, it's partly why."

"And what is the other part?"

"Last night when Carol was singing I saw you there. I didn't mean to stare."

"It was foolish of me to go," the woman said. "Sentimental. I've sat around so many campfires with Paul—my husband. He had a good voice and he liked to sing those songs your sister was singing last night. I shouldn't have gone. It made me miss him too much. I don't really want to remember."

Jenny could better understand her weeping now. Of course those songs would make her cry. They both sat quietly for a time, with no need to chatter. Greg had said that Señora Consuelo had lost her husband only six months ago. What would it be like to lose someone you loved? Jenny wondered. What if she, Jenny Hanford, lost her father or mother or sister? It was a frightening thought, and she put it away from her. She didn't want to understand enough to make such a thought seem real.

It was strange, she was discovering, but she no longer felt awkward about talking to this woman. Consuelo Eliot did not seem like a stranger anymore. Not a friend, but not wholly a stranger either. She was more like a listening presence. Jenny sensed that she would listen and would not laugh or mock or disapprove.

"Tell me about the yellow smock," Señora Consuelo said.

That was hard to do, since Jenny was not sure she understood her own feeling about the smock. Señora Consuelo had said she didn't want to remember. But

Jenny felt differently, and she spoke with hesitation.

"I think I'll always want to remember everything. When I went into that little house where you lived I didn't know it had belonged to you. But I had a feeling that whoever you were, when you went away you left the smock there so the house wouldn't be empty, and you left the calendar on the wall so the house would remember the day of your going. I think you must have liked that little place very much. But I don't know why the penny was in the pocket."

The woman's mouth twisted as though in pain and she closed her eyes. When she began to speak she did not open them, and Jenny had the feeling that she was talking more to herself than to any listener.

"Paul and I had been married only a few months. We wanted our own home, and this land below Haunted Mesa seemed the right place for a ranch. We were happy living in that rough little cabin while this house was being built. When we left it I wondered if I could ever be as happy as that again." She paused, once more lost in her own thoughts.

"Were you?" Jenny asked.

"Of course. But in a different way. Things change, people change. One can't remain forever young."

Jenny waited silently. It seemed to her that being young was endless. It took forever to grow up.

After a moment Señora Consuelo moved restlessly and opened her eyes to regard Jenny with a look that seemed once more cool and remote.

"When one is young and has lost nothing, it's pleasant to remember. But when you've lost everything, all remembering is too painful. I prefer apathy."

Apathy meant doing nothing, Jenny thought. It was a word Dad had used briefly to her when she had started failing in school. It was a not-caring sort of feeling with no happiness in it. Somehow she had emerged from it a little since she had come to the ranch. She was beginning to feel angry and rebellious—as though maybe she could do something herself, after all, and stop being a shadow for Carol Hanford. But there were dangers hidden in this new feeling, and trouble might lie ahead.

Señora Consuelo got up with nervous impatience and walked around the room as though she could not sit still for a moment longer. Her rust-colored robe flowed about her as she moved. Once she stopped before a shelf on which had been placed a row of strange Indian figures. They were like dolls, some of them with masks, or with horns on their heads, and their hands raised. She picked up one doll and looked at it closely before she replaced it on the shelf.

"Why did you really come here to my house?" she asked abruptly.

The question took Jenny by surprise, but she tried to answer honestly because this was a woman who demanded honesty. "In the beginning it was because Greg—he's a boy I met at the campfire last night— said I should do something unexpected, even if I got into trouble. Then perhaps people would pay attention to me, instead of always to Carol. So I thought I'd come here and—and break the rules. But after I saw the cabin and Greg told me something about you, I only wanted to see where you lived. Maybe to see you again. But I didn't mean to go beyond the gate."

The woman turned slowly and looked at Jenny for a moment. "I'll tell you about the penny," she said. "An Indian head, wasn't it? For some reason it was my lucky piece. I suppose I felt that if I left it there in the pocket of a smock I'd worn happily so often in that very cabin, it would make a sort of continuity—make a thread between the woman I was going to become when I moved away and came to live with Paul in this house and the woman I had been as a young bride. Imagine! I could do silly young things like that in those days."

"Did you ever go back to the cabin?" Jenny asked.

"Once in a while in the beginning. I had to let it know that I hadn't forgotten my happiness there. The smock kept the place from feeling empty to me, even though the calendar made a sort of period to mark the end of that part of my life. When Paul and I gave this place to the university we made it a stipulation that the cabin was not to be torn down while we lived."

"It needs to be cleaned," Jenny said. "It's full of dust and cobwebs."

"I haven't been back for a long time." She spoke almost apologetically, as though Jenny had made her feel guilty about forgetting the cabin.

There was silence again, while Señora Consuelo roamed her big living room, absently touching an ornament here, standing before a picture there.

This was the strangest conversation she had ever had, Jenny thought. It was as though this woman, who had lived a very long time, and Jenny Hanford, who had lived comparatively few years, had made some sort of bridge between them, where neither was young or old. They were just two people who could talk to each other. Perhaps it was because neither knew the other well and didn't expect certain things of the other person. Jenny found that she was mildly curious about what would happen next in this strange situation, but she no longer felt any anxiety, no longer felt apologetic.

Because Señora Consuelo had paused before the painting of Haunted Mesa, Jenny asked the same question she had asked of Greg last night.

"Why is it called Haunted Mesa?"

For the first time the woman almost smiled as she turned away from the painting and looked at Jenny. It was as though this was a topic to interest her and in which there was no dangerous pain.

"There used to be a pueblo near here before the Spaniards came," she said. "A small Zuñi pueblo. The people were peaceful farmers, they warred with no one. When the Spaniards came the Zuñis submitted to their rule—for a time. Then there was an uprising of all the pueblos and the Spaniards were driven out. Though not for long. Diego de Vargas led a force up from El Paso, and he began to subdue the pueblos one by one. Rather than be conquered again, the people of this pueblo fled to the top of the mesa. They fortified themselves up there and built shelters and a kiva where they could meet and hold their ceremonies. Sometimes they would come down at night and steal from the Spaniards to keep themselves alive. Some of them starved to death but some lived, and eventually those who remained settled elsewhere with other Zuñis."

Jenny left her chair and went to stand before a window where she could look out at the real mesa, instead of at a painting. She liked to think of those Indian men and women who didn't want to be conquered and who took refuge up there and held off the Spaniards.

"Sometimes I can still feel the war inside me," Señora Consuelo said.

Jenny waited, not knowing what she meant.

"My grandparents came here from Mexico," the woman went on. "Some of their ancestors were those very Spaniards who came to conquer the New World. Others were Aztec Indians. The sons of Montezuma! My father was so terribly Spanish you'd have thought he came here straight from Madrid. He wanted only to be Spanish and to forget about Mexico and the Indians. He wasn't happy when I married an Anglo—Paul Eliot. So there has been something of a war inside me as to who I am—Mexican, Spanish, Indian, American."

"Who won?" Jenny asked.

When the Señora really smiled she was very beautiful and her face lost some of the down-drooping lines. "We all did. I like being some of everything. Perhaps that's what being an American is all about. But because of my husband I've given myself mainly to working for the Indians. It was what he cared most about, and I came to care too. I used to go everywhere with him when he was gathering material for a book. I've lived in hogans and tepees and pueblos. But I always had this house to come home to—and the ranch, and our quiet life here while Paul wrote his books."

In spite of herself, Señora Consuelo *was* remembering, Jenny thought, and she grew a little afraid. Because the pain might come slashing back when she remembered her loss again.

"Should anybody be up on top of the mesa now?" Jenny asked, trying to distract her.

There was a thoughtful look in Señora Consuelo's eyes as she came to sit on the moss-green sofa opposite Jenny.

"Why do you ask that?"

"Last night I thought I saw something moving up there against the sky. And today I saw something again. I'm not sure what."

The Señora nodded. "Yes. I saw it last night too and I wondered if it could be some animal—a coyote perhaps, though there aren't many left around here anymore. Surely no one from the ranch would be up there at night."

Jenny felt relieved. Now she didn't have to wonder whether what she had seen was only her imagination.

"Of course," Señora Consuelo went on, "there's a legend of Indian ghosts on the mountain. People claim to have seen spirits up there. And sometimes when the moon is full, they say you can hear their drums or see the smoke from their juniper fires."

"Have you seen them? Have you heard the drums?"

"I'm afraid not. Though I've looked and listened often. I'd love to believe in those old stories."

"Perhaps that's what we did see."

"Perhaps."

This time the silence was like an ending, and Jenny sensed that she must not stay any longer. "I— I'd better go back to our cottage now. My mother will be wondering where I am."

"If you must. I haven't been a very good hostess, have I? I haven't offered you a glass of lemonade, or some of the honey-ginger cookies I've taught Maria to make. So you'll have to come again."

"Could I?" Jenny asked eagerly. "Could I really come again?"

Señora Consuelo stood up and held out her hand. "The way you say that pleases me. I'm not sure I deserve it. I apologize for not welcoming you more quickly. Perhaps you are my goodluck penny for today."

Jenny took her hand awkwardly, feeling self-conscious for the first time. Señora Consuelo came with her to the door and stood there until Jenny had gone out through the blue gate.

Once she was away from the house she began to run, forgetting about the altitude that could make one breathless, and hurried through the door of Juniper to hug her startled mother.

"I've had such an exciting time!" she cried.

Her mother loosed her clinging arms gently and shook her head. "Not now, dear," she warned, and Jenny realized that she had plunged into an atmosphere of even more tension than usual. Carol, slim in jeans and a red blouse, sat on the bed in their parents' room, looking very calm and determined. Dad must have finished his class for the morning, because he stood leaning against the bureau, while Mother sat in the one chair, looking unhappy.

"What's happened?" Jenny asked.

"Don't interrupt," Dad said and went on talking to Carol as he had been when Jenny dashed into the room. "You absolutely cannot give a concert in Santa Fe," he said. "And I don't care who wants you to. That's not why we came here—so you could perform. This is supposed to be a vacation."

"I don't want a vacation," Carol said.

Jenny didn't need to hear any more. She went into the other room, which she shared with Carol, and closed the door. Then she looked for the carved figure of the roadrunner she had left on her pillow. Ever since she had bought it she had liked to hold the piece of carving and run her fingers over the smooth pale wood when she was upset about something. It seemed to soothe her. But the roadrunner was gone from her pillow.

She wanted to burst into that room again and demand whether anyone had taken the little carved figure, but she knew better. So instead she threw herself down on the bed, feeling upset and angry and confused. She had wanted someone to talk to, someone she could tell about her fabulous morning. Things like getting to meet Consuelo Eliot didn't happen every day. And there wasn't anyone to talk to. Not anyone at all.

She pounded the pillow under her head, feeling very, very sorry for Jenny Hanford. And thoroughly angry with the world.

4. The Boy
in the Window

The Hanfords were anything but cheerful at lunch-time. It was a special lunch too, of Mexican food. Usually they all liked chili and frijoles, but no one was hungry today. They sat at their small table, apart from the rest of the conference, and hardly said a word. Carol looked calm but far away, as though she could not be reached, and Mother had been crying. Clearly Dad was still seething. He had pointed out that Carol was not yet of age and that she would have to do as her parents said. Carol behaved as though she had gone suddenly deaf and couldn't hear the voices around her. So everyone had given up talking.

Once Jenny had tried to ask about the roadrunner, but such nonsense had been brushed aside. The carving had not turned up, though by now Jenny had searched every inch of her room and her parents' room as well. She had even crawled under their bed while they were arguing, and no one had noticed.

She hated to see Carol and their parents so far apart. From her own position on the edge of all this tension, she could understand how each one felt, but she didn't want to take sides. When the painful silence grew too long, she made an effort to break it, simply because she couldn't bear it any longer.

"Have you ever heard of Paul Eliot?" she asked her father, sounding more abrupt than she intended. But at least she had caught his attention.

He glanced at her in surprise. "Of course I have. I've read a number of his books. Perhaps he understood the Indians better than most white men ever have. His death was an American loss."

"Did you know that he lived here at the ranch?"

"Yes, I've known that for a long time." Dad seemed almost relieved to be thinking about something besides Carol. "A year ago when I signed up to teach at this conference, he was still alive, and your mother and I had planned to look him up while we were here. When he wrote about Indians, he often wrote about ecology too, since the Indian has understood the balance of nature and the protection of her resources far better than the white man ever has. I had hoped we might have something in common."

"His wife is still here," Jenny said.

"I know. I was inquiring about her yesterday. We'd have liked to pay her a visit, but I understand she has been ill and hasn't been seeing anyone."

"I saw her this morning," Jenny said.

Mother looked up from the chili she wasn't eating. "How did that happen?"

"I was looking at her house. It's a very interesting house—adobe, with blue trim around the windows and a blue gate. She came to the door while I was there."

"Oh, dear," Mother said. "I hope you didn't stare

at her. You do get terribly interested in people sometimes, and I know you don't mean to offend, but—"

"I don't think I offended her," Jenny said. "But I got to talk to her for a while."

Both Mother and Dad looked at her now, staring a little themselves.

"Now, Jenny," Mother said, "we've all been asked—everyone at the Center has been asked—not to disturb Mrs. Eliot. The poor woman doesn't want to see strangers or be bothered in any way."

"She invited me into her house," Jenny said, "and we talked for a long time."

All three stared at her now. Carol, who had been lost in her own world, her own problems, had suddenly become aware that the focus had moved away from her, and she looked a bit surprised.

Dad began to laugh, sounding more cheerful than he had since they had come to the ranch. "So our Jenny has been the one to gain entry to forbidden ground! Perhaps you'll introduce me to your new friend sometime?"

"Oh, no!" Mother cried. "Jenny must have pushed her way in, and the poor woman couldn't do anything else, without being rude, but invite her inside."

"I didn't push my way in! And she wouldn't have minded being rude if she felt like it," Jenny said indignantly. "But she was interested in me. She talked to me. And she listened too."

"Well, you're not to go near her again," Mother said. "I won't have my daughter bothering that poor woman."

"She's not a 'poor woman'!" Jenny cried, her indignation growing. "I thought she was wonderful. And she invited me back. Her house is beautiful inside. I never saw a house like it. There were those brown viga beams across the ceiling, and all sorts of paintings and books, and—"

"This afternoon," Carol broke in, "I am going to take the car the Center sends to Santa Fe. If I can, I'll come back in the evening. I've got to make arrangements for the concert. They said I could hold it at their wonderful opera house."

Mother and Dad looked at each other and seemed to exchange a signal before they turned back to Jenny. "Tell me more about Mrs. Eliot's house," Dad said.

Carol looked so shocked that Jenny felt almost sorry for her. She was used to having the world revolve around her and she didn't always remember that other people existed. Anyway, Jenny meant to take advantage of this unusual attention. She told them more about the adobe house and of what Consuelo Eliot was like, though a few things she kept to herself. She did not want to tell anyone about Señora Consuelo's feelings for the cabin where she had lived and where she had left a yellow smock hanging on a hook. Jenny sensed that those things belonged privately between Señora Consuelo and herself. But there was quite a lot more to tell and she enjoyed the novelty of having her parents take the time away from Carol to listen.

She felt hungrier now, and she managed to savor the chili and beans while she talked. After a while Mother began to eat too. Carol paid no attention to her food. She just sat and listened, and Jenny wondered how a performer felt when she knew she had lost her audience. It wasn't possible not to feel a mean little triumph, but she would try to make it up to Carol later. Right now she liked what was happening.

When they left the dining hall, she found Greg waiting for her outside, and she stayed behind as the rest of the family went off.

"You sure were talking a lot at lunch," Greg said, as they walked in the direction of the cottages. "I looked around at you a couple of times and everybody was paying you plenty of attention. What did you do?"

She returned his grin. "I suppose I've been doing what you told me to. Except that I didn't get into any trouble. It all turned out fine, and I really had something interesting to talk about."

"Tell me about it," he said as they walked along.

He was more like the boy she had seen last night, but she did not want to tell him of how Señora Consuelo had felt about that yellow smock, or about some of the other things she had said. However, she could tell him something of the same story she had related to her parents. And Greg too listened.

"'Wow!" he said when she finished. "You really have had an interesting morning."

"Only one thing has happened that I don't like," Jenny said. "When we drove up from Santa Fe, we stopped at a village where there were wood-carvers, and I bought something in one of the shops. It was a little roadrunner carved from wood. This morning it disappeared, and I can't find it anywhere."

They had reached Juniper and Aspen, and suddenly Greg hung back, his expression odd and a little shamefaced.

"I'm sorry," he said. "You wanted something exciting to happen, so I thought I'd help you out."

"You mean you took my carving?" Jenny asked in astonishment.

He grinned at her sheepishly. "It would have been a mystery, wouldn't it? Something for you to think about. And in a little while I'd have given it back. But you'd have had some excitement for a while, the way you wanted. Only now you don't need that kind of excitement after all that's been happening to you."

"You can give it back right now," Jenny said, feeling thoroughly annoyed. "I don't think that was a good idea at all. Anyway, how could you take it when everyone was there in the cottage?"

"They were all talking in the next room and sounding pretty excited. Your window was open and I could see that carving on the pillow. I guessed it was yours. So I went through the window and took it. But I've got it in my room, and I'll give it back to you right away."

Jenny followed him a bit grumpily into his cottage. Aspen was laid out in the same pattern as Juniper. First a little hall that ended with the bathroom between the two bedrooms—one on the right and one on the left. Greg said his parents were out, and he went into the left-hand room, walking to the small maple dresser to look at the top where he had strewn some of his possessions. Jenny stayed in the doorway, watching. For a moment he felt all around on top of the dresser and then turned to face her, looking puzzled.

"That's funny. I'm sure I put it right here, but it's not here now."

Jenny waited in the doorway. He would find it, of course. He had to. She was still annoyed with him, but he must have put it somewhere else and when she had it back perhaps she would forgive him.

After a moment of fruitless searching, he paused beside a small table where several books were piled.

"Something else is gone. At lunchtime I asked one of the girls over at the dining hall to fix me some sandwiches. I thought I might go over to Finger Rocks this afternoon, and I knew I'd be hungry before I got home. So I brought the box back with me and put it right here on this table. And it's gone too."

Jenny came into the room and looked around. There weren't many hiding places, and the roadrunner was nowhere to be seen. Nor could she see the lunch box. But she did notice something else. From among the books she picked up an odd-shaped piece of wood and held it out to Greg.

"What's this?"

He took it from her hand and studied it in surprise. It seemed to be the rough carving of a snake. The slim body rippled in rather flat curves, and the head was slightly raised, with the eyes indicated and a tiny tongue barely protruding from the mouth.

"I don't know what it is," Greg said. "I never saw it before."

But the roadrunner was more important to Jenny

than the snake. "I don't think you should have taken it," she said.

"How was I to know it was going to disappear right out of my room, along with my lunch box? Something funny is going on around here, and I want to know what it is." That chip on Greg's shoulder was very noticeable, and he was sounding belligerent.

From across the little hall there came a sound like a window being opened. For an instant Greg and Jenny stared at each other. Then he ran across to his parents' room, and Jenny followed. They were just in time to see the boy poised on the windowsill as he climbed through.

For a moment Greg and Jenny were both too startled to move. As they hesitated, the boy in the window threw something at them and dropped out of sight in one fluid movement. They heard the thud as he reached the ground outside.

Greg was after him at once, climbing through the window, but Jenny stopped because there on the rag rug at her feet lay the roadrunner, where the boy had thrown it. She bent to pick it up and examined it carefully. No damage seemed to have been done. When she was sure of that, she went out through the door and found Greg standing between the two cottages looking around angrily.

"He went off like the wind," Greg said. "And he had that box with my lunch under his arm. He lost himself among the cottages and just disappeared. There's no chance of catching him now. He could have gone in any direction. But it looks as though there's a thief on the grounds. We've got to do something."

"At least I've got my roadrunner back," Jenny said.

Greg looked off at the great mesa with its high crown of rock, standing almost shadowless in the noontime sun.

"I'll bet he's gone up there," he said. "Did you get a good look at him?"

"I guess so. I mean I think I'd recognize him if I saw him again."

"Tell me what he looked like," Greg said.

Jenny glanced at him in surprise. "Why, he was— just a boy. He had rather long black hair and sort of dark skin. Maybe like an Indian."

Greg nodded. "That's right. I think he *was* an Indian."

"Perhaps he works around the ranch," Jenny said. "We could ask. Maybe we could find out who he is and talk to him."

"There aren't any Indians around the ranch. There's no pueblo near here, so they don't get Indians applying for jobs. I was talking to one of the corral hands about that. Mostly the people around here are Chicanos—Mexican Americans. There aren't any Indians."

"But that boy—"

"Was an Indian. Sure. And he's got to be caught and stopped from stealing. People don't take my things and get away with it! Look, Jenny, I know a place where we can see the mesa close up. You want to come along?"

He sounded pretty mad and she hesitated uncomfortably. She wanted to know more about what was happening, but somehow she had felt a stab of sympathy for that boy. For just a moment, while he was still in the window, she had seen his eyes and they looked frightened.

"Anyway, I'm going up where I can have a better look," Greg said.

She didn't want him to go alone. If he meant to catch this boy, she wanted to be there, though she wasn't quite sure why.

"Why do you think he'd be hiding up on the mesa?" she asked.

"Well—it would be a good place. After you told me last night about seeing something move up there, I started watching. And this morning I think I saw someone up there myself. Just for a second. I didn't get a very good look."

"Someone with a blue head?" Jenny asked.

"No, of course not. With a head like anybody else. What are you talking about?"

She told him about the strange figure she had seen, and he whistled in wonderment. "Maybe we'd better tell somebody. After all, he was stealing here at the Center."

"Only food," Jenny said. "He gave my roadrunner back." She patted the pocket in her jeans where she had put it. "Maybe he left that carved snake behind as a—a sort of exchange for your lunch box."

Greg snorted in scorn. "Some exchange! Nobody's going to steal from me!"

He was already leading the way up the small hill that rose directly behind the cottages, and Jenny followed him, feeling increasingly uneasy. She wasn't always sure that she liked Greg. He could be a little too belligerent at times.

After a few minutes of climbing up a steep dirt path, they reached a broad plateau, where they were high enough to look down upon the entire complex of conference buildings and cottages. Directly overhead the sun was hot, yet there was a breeze, and because of the altitude it wasn't unbearably warm. As she turned around to look toward the mesa, she could see a long, low wooden building built on this same level, where it could face the mountain. Beyond it, the land dipped into an arroyo, from which Haunted Mesa rose straight up in all its great mass.

"I don't see him anywhere," Greg said. "But if there's a thief around, we'd better report it."

"Can't we wait a little?" Jenny asked. "Maybe he isn't really a thief. Maybe he was only hungry."

"Then why doesn't he come to the Center and ask for something to eat? They'd give him food, and help him if he needs help."

"Perhaps there's some reason we don't understand," Jenny said. "After all, you took something too this morning, but I'm not going to report you, or call you a thief."

He grinned sheepishly. "Okay. But this is different, and I don't like people who try to get away with stealing from me. Let's walk to that building over there."

"What is it?" Jenny asked as they followed a winding road that climbed up from the conference grounds.

"It's an outdoor meeting room where small groups can come. The windows don't have any glass, and you can be practically outside, but under shelter from the sun."

Jenny studied the small building as they followed the road toward it. "I think there's somebody in there now." She could see a solitary figure sitting at a table facing the mesa. The person had blond hair flowing to the shoulders, but from the back she wasn't sure whether it was a man or a woman.

"Sure," Greg said. "That's my mother. She said she was going to sketch the mesa this morning."

"Is she an artist?"

"She does illustrations for children's books."

"What does your father do?"

"He works for a bank in Philadelphia, where we live, but he's tired of it, and he's got this new bug about ecology. So maybe we're going to come out here to New Mexico to live. He'd like to buy a ranch, so we came out to look around. And he wanted to take that course your father's teaching at the Center."

"It might be fun to live out here."

"Yeah, I guess so." Greg didn't sound altogether sure.

As they approached the structure, Jenny saw that it was built like a train coach, long and narrow, with entrances at each end. Wooden chairs with desk arms had been set about informally, along with two or three small tables. At one of these Mrs. Frost sat with a sketch block before her. She looked up smiling as they came in. She seemed nice, Jenny thought, with her long straight hair and tanned skin, and there were little crinkles at the corners of her eyes, as though she laughed a lot.

"'Hi," she said as Greg and Jenny stepped into the room.

Greg pushed Jenny ahead of him. "This is Jenny Hanford," he told his mother.

Mrs. Frost smiled. "Hello, Jenny. Greg was telling me about you. I'm glad he has found a young friend. My husband has been enjoying your father's course."

Not a word about Carol. Jenny found herself returning the warm smile.

"Come and see, if you like," Mrs. Frost said and pushed the sketch block toward them.

They stood beside her and Jenny looked at the pencil drawing. Even though it wasn't in color, Greg's mother had caught the almost frighteningly steep pitch of the rock as it rose in ramparts near the top. Jenny looked from the sketch to the real mountain.

From this vantage point she could see through the open windows and across the arroyo that dipped below the plateau, right to where the mountain began. The lower slopes were not so steep as the upper, and were made up of earth and loose rock, which would clearly be dangerous to climb because it would crumble and slide beneath your feet. Where the gentler slope ended, higher up, there were only some straight pinnacles of rock.

"How do you two feel about the mountain?" Mrs. Frost asked.

It was a strange question, but Greg tried to answer it. "It makes me want to climb up there. From the top I'd own the whole world."

His mother smiled. "And you, Jenny?"

"I don't know—maybe it scares me a little."

"In what way?"

"It's been there so long. All those millions of years. It remembers the Indians who died up there because they wanted to stay free. It's as though it knows everything there is to know—past and future."

Mrs. Frost nodded, pleased. "Yes. There's a sense of enormous power about it. We're so little that it could conquer and crush us in an instant."

"That's why I'd like to go up on top," Greg said. "I'd like to show the mountain that it can't conquer me."

"It's not necessary to prove yourself all the time," his mother said gently.

There was an awkward moment and Jenny sensed a resentment in Greg. "It looks as if there's no way up," she said, breaking the small silence.

"There's a way." Greg pointed. "You can follow the arroyo toward that deep cut at the far end of the mountain. There's a sort of crevice in the rock down there, where you can climb up. Mom, you didn't happen to see anybody go by while you were working here, did you?"

"As a matter of fact, I did," she said. "I saw a boy go down into the arroyo. He was running when I saw him, and I wondered where he was going. I supposed he was someone from the ranch—perhaps Mexican or Indian."

Greg glanced at Jenny, but he didn't say anything about the boy. "Let's go down there and have a look," he said.

She didn't want to explore any farther, but neither did she want Greg to come upon the Indian boy when he was alone, because she wasn't at all sure what Greg would do. And she felt an increasing sympathy for the boy. If he was really hiding out on the mesa, something must be terribly wrong.

"All right," she said. And then to Mrs. Frost, "I like your drawing. Are you going to use it in a book?"

"Perhaps," Mrs. Frost said. "Greg, you won't try to climb the mesa, will you?"

"No, I won't. Not until someone who knows the way is along."

She seemed satisfied with his promise and picked up her pencil again. Jenny followed Greg out the door, and in moments they were scrambling down the slope into the gully which was called an arroyo and had been made by water rushing down the mountain. There was more vegetation there— junipers, cottonwoods, and a few scraggly evergreens, as well as some low bushes.

"You have to stay out of this sort of place when there's any chance of rain," Greg said. "Dad says there isn't much rain in the Southwest, but when there is, it can be a cloudburst and water pours down every ditch. Cars have been swept away when they were caught in canyons, and people have drowned."

Jenny looked up at the vast blue of the sky, but only a few white clouds were visible.

In the dry bottom of the ditch they could walk along almost as if they followed a road. At the far end, the arroyo rose toward a deep fold in the mountain. Nothing was to be seen, nothing moved, and there was no breeze down here. Jenny began to feel hot and dusty.

"What are we looking for?" she asked. "If the boy went along here, he could be up on top by now."

Greg stopped and gazed upward at the great rock ramparts that towered over them. "I don't know. I thought we might find something. Some sort of—well, clue."

"Your mother saw him go by. That seems like clue enough," Jenny said. "I think I'll go back now."

She was no longer worried about Greg's meeting the boy, and this wild area made her uneasy. The Conference Center was out of sight, except for that one low building where Greg's mother sat working. And some of the time the twisted cottonwoods hid that as well. She had a strong feeling that she wanted to return to where there were people around, instead of only the spirits of that powerful mountain.

"Go ahead," Greg said. "I like it here. I think I'll stay a while. But I wish I had that box of sandwiches."

Jenny started up the side of the arroyo, using juniper branches to pull herself along. When she was near the top of the bank, she paused to look down at Greg. He hadn't moved, but was still staring up at the mesa. She called down to him.

"If you found that boy, what would you do?"

He did not turn his head. "I'd fix him. Nobody gets away with that sort of stuff with me!"

She did not like the threat in his voice, but he wouldn't find the boy now. She started across the little plateau that would take her back to the conference buildings, reminding herself that this was not a "plateau" out here. It was a smaller mesa.

She skirted the long room where Mrs. Frost sat

sketching and took the shortcut downhill to return to Juniper. Even before she reached the cottage, she could hear her father's voice, and she knew he was angry with Carol all over again.

5. The Road to Santa Fe

When Jenny stepped into the little hallway, she could look through the door and see her mother lying on her bed with a wet cloth on her forehead. Dad was raging around the small room as if he found it a cage, and Jenny gathered from his words that Carol had given them the slip and gone to Santa Fe.

"I'm going after her!" he was saying. "I don't have a class this afternoon, so I'm going to take the car and go after her. She left you the name of the people she's going to see in Santa Fe, didn't she?"

Mother moaned softly and murmured that the name was in her purse. Dad went to the bureau and dumped everything out of the handbag. He was in a real temper. Jenny started to tiptoe away to her own room, when he looked up and saw her.

"Come in here," he said.

She went to the doorway and looked worriedly at her mother. Dad found the slip of paper and waved it triumphantly. "Here we are. It's an address on Camino del Monte Sol. I'll be on my way."

"I suppose you'll have to go," Mother murmured

from the bed, "but perhaps you should help her. Let her do what she wants. She's an adult now, and—"

"She's not an adult till she gets some sense," Dad broke in.

Mother went right on, though her voice was faint. "If she gets this concert out of her system, she may be more willing to think about college. Right now we've driven her into running off."

Dad shook his head helplessly, but his anger was quieting. "After the concert, there'll just be something else. There always is."

Jenny felt sorry for them both. Having a prodigy in the family was difficult for them all.

"I'll think about it on the drive to Santa Fe," he said. Then he turned to Jenny. "Your mother's feeling ill. Stay nearby, will you, in case she wants anything."

"All right," Jenny said, but Mother raised herself on one elbow, wincing as the pain increased.

"No, Roy. I don't need to be looked after, and I don't want to be worried about. I'll just be quiet and try to sleep. Take Jenny with you, if she wants to go. She ought to see more of Santa Fe, and I'm sure she'd like the trip. Wouldn't you, Jenny?"

She wouldn't like this particular trip at all, Jenny thought, but her mother was staring at her intensely, and she knew that look meant she was to say "yes." Perhaps her mother felt that she might be of some help with Carol, though Jenny didn't see how. She nodded reluctantly.

Mother dropped back onto the pillow, and Dad bent to kiss her cheek. Then he went out of the cottage, Jenny trailing after him as he marched toward the parking lot where all the cars at the Center were kept.

It wasn't far and he didn't speak on the way. She knew he was still seething, and she only wished she were older so that she could say something sensible and calming. This was going to be a painful trip, and she hated to think of what might happen at the other end when they found Carol.

When they reached the lot, Dad started across it with long strides, while Jenny hurried in his wake. Their blue Mustang was parked near a corner and, as they headed toward it, a tall woman in well-cut gray slacks and a blue blouse got out of a nearby car and slammed the door. It was Señora Consuelo.

Dad went past her without noticing, but Jenny paused.

"Hello, Jenny," the woman said. "Is that your father? I wonder if he knows anything about cars? I've been having trouble, and I have an appointment in Santa Fe this afternoon. I left the car here, instead of in my garage, so I'd be near people if it wouldn't start."

Dad heard and turned around. He couldn't entirely stifle his impatience, but he was naturally courteous, and he offered help.

"I'm not much good at cars," he said. "But if you're going to Santa Fe, I can give you a lift." He was already opening the Mustang's door.

"Thank you," Señora Consuelo said, but she hadn't missed the suppressed impatience. "I don't want to be any trouble. You're Jenny's father, aren't you? I'm Consuelo Eliot."

"I'm sorry," he said. "I didn't mean to be brusque.

My older daughter is getting herself into some sort of jam, and I've got to get to Santa Fe to see what's happening. Please come with us. We can bring you back if you're not staying over."

She accepted graciously, but when he went around to open the front door on the passenger's side, she shook her head. "Why don't you let Jenny and me sit in back? I'm sure you don't want to talk to anyone just now, and Jenny and I are friends."

Dad's look told her he was grateful for her understanding. A moment later they were in the back seat and he was turning the car out of the parking lot.

Señora Consuelo put her woven Mexican handbag on the seat beside her and smiled at Jenny as the car took the paved road out to the highway. Her black hair with its silver streakings was brushed into a crest above her forehead, and she wore silver-and-turquoise earrings with a coral-and-black inlay. When she spoke her voice was low, so as not to disturb Dad, who was concentrating on his own problems.

"Perhaps I have you to thank, Jenny, for making me decide on this trip today. This morning you jolted me out of my state of doing nothing. I haven't been to Santa Fe since Paul died. It's time I went."

"I never meant to jolt you," Jenny said.

Señora Consuelo smiled. "I'm glad you did. After you'd gone, I decided that I was going to get in touch with life again. Which is what Paul would want me to do. So I accepted this invitation to Santa Fe. I thank you, Jenny Hanford."

Jenny experienced an unexpected surge of happiness. She didn't entirely understand what had happened, but she felt glad that it had.

"When Paul and I came here to Haunted Mesa Ranch, there was only a dirt road out to the highway," Señora Consuelo went on. "In fact, there wasn't any highway—just another dirt road that connected with the road to Santa Fe. When it rained, it was quite usual to get stuck in the mud. It took hours to get to Santa Fe, so we didn't go often."

Because of Señora Consuelo's company, the trip did not seem as long and boring as it might have otherwise. Jenny wanted to tell her about what had happened in Juniper cottage that morning, and about the frightened Indian boy who had taken Greg's lunch box, but somehow she held back. She didn't know Señora Consuelo all that well, and she wasn't sure how the señora might feel about a thief on the premises. So mostly she listened and found herself interested.

Señora Consuelo explained that she was going into town to see an old friend of her husband's. "His name is Jim Kingsley. He's a retired anthropologist who has worked among the Pueblo Indians for years. He is older than Paul was and he taught us both a great deal. He's respected in Washington and he goes there once in a while to pound on a few tables and try to talk sense to those who don't know anything firsthand about Indians."

Jenny wondered what would happen if she said, I think there's an Indian boy hiding up on the mesa, but she couldn't bring herself to say it. Not yet.

Señora Consuelo went on, speaking as if Jenny were grown-up. "One reason we thought so highly of

Jim Kingsley is that he has never made the two great mistakes of most white men. He doesn't treat Indians as though they were small children who don't know how to conduct their own affairs, or know what is good for them. But neither does he try to turn them into white men. He thinks they should make their own choices, just as other Americans do."

Jenny watched Señora Consuelo's face glow as she talked, and was happy to see the way she had come to life. Jenny had thought her beautiful last night when she had seen her standing in the light from the campfire, but she was much more beautiful now, with this warmth in her eyes and a sense of excitement in her speech. This was a woman who had spent much of her life really caring about other people.

"It isn't the business of government to make everyone be exactly like everyone else," Señora Consuelo went on. "We should all have the same opportunities and privileges without intolerance toward each other; but the Irish should be allowed to be Irish; Jews, Jews; black people, black; and Italians, Italians. The same with all the rest, if that's what they want."

"But doesn't that divide everybody?" Jenny puzzled.

"It shouldn't. We're all Americans together, but we mustn't lose the wonderful treasure of our different cultures. Each one enriches us all, and that's what America is all about. There were terrible early years of closed reservations and virtual isolation for the Indians. Then the United States Government reversed that and for all too long decided that the solution to the problems of the Indians was to force them into the mainstream of American life and make them forget all about being Indians. Of course it never worked, and now we're changing that approach. We'd better change, because the young Indians are acquiring a voice, and they aren't going to take injustice as meekly as their fathers and grandfathers did."

She broke off and smiled apologetically. "There—I'm lecturing you! I used to do that, you know. I mean I used to give talks at schools and universities and women's clubs."

"I should think you could do a lot of good," Jenny said. "You'd make people listen to you." She wished she knew a little more about that Indian boy with the frightened eyes—the boy who had run away in fear and might be hiding on the mesa. She would like to talk to this woman about him. But she would have to know more first.

Her companion was quiet for a time, and the sadness was there again. Jenny thought she might be remembering other trips she had made with her husband over this road.

A thought had begun to burgeon at the back of Jenny's mind. A possibility, if she dared to carry it out. She wondered how she could ask Señora Consuelo, and whether she would be willing to do what Jenny wanted to suggest.

Up in front, Dad was still silent, lost in his own worry about Carol. At another time he would have wanted to talk to Consuelo Eliot himself. Perhaps they could talk on the way home. Unless Carol—but Jenny didn't want to think about that. She couldn't do anything about her sister now. She was just being carried along in this car to whatever disasters lay ahead.

Now and then as the car sped on, Señora Consuelo would point out something interesting along the road.

"That's San Angelo Pueblo over there," she said as they passed a side road leading to a clump of cube-like sandstone houses. "The Indians who live there are Zuñis. Most Zuñis live farther west in a place called Zuñi, but there are a few here. Pueblo Indians aren't divided into tribes, like the Navahos and others. They consist of small groups who live in villages and are called by special names. Are you interested in any of this, Jenny?"

Jenny nodded. She had a special interest in Indians right now. One Indian. "We studied about them in school when I was younger, but somehow it wasn't as real as it seems now."

Señora Consuelo touched her earrings. "These are Zuñi work. They do beautiful things with silver and turquoise, and bits of coral and jet. There are a lot of cheap imitations now, and the art and original crafts of the Indians are being lost forever. We mustn't let that happen."

They had reached the highway that ran north to Taos and south to Santa Fe, and part of the time they were traveling along the banks of the Rio Grande, with the water flowing beside the road, greenish in the afternoon sun. The miles ran away beneath the wheels of the car, and Jenny still hadn't settled in her mind the thing she wanted to ask of Señora Consuelo. But now they were passing the huge Camel Rock beside the road, and she knew they were nearing Santa Fe, so she put aside thinking about her plan for now.

"I've always loved this town," Señora Consuelo said as they reached the outskirts. "It's like me—a mixture of cultures. Spanish, Indian, Anglo—all living together fairly well. It's a town of artists, writers, musicians, and other creative people. Scientists too, because Los Alamos isn't far away. But I've never been here without Paul, so it's full of memories. I wish you could have known my husband, Jenny."

In the front seat, Dad stirred. "Where would you like me to drop you, Mrs. Eliot?"

"I'm going to a house on Canyon Road," Señora Consuelo said, "if that's convenient for you."

"Of course," Dad said. "Will you tell me how to get there?" Señora Consuelo directed him and eventually they turned up a narrow road that ran along the spine of a hill. Artists' studios lined the sidewalk and there were all sorts of fascinating shops. When Dad stopped his car at the indicated place, she put a hand on the door and then paused.

"Don't get out, Mr. Hanford. I can manage. And I'll stay right here until you return. Would you mind if Jenny came with me? I think she'd be interested in this place."

Dad smiled over his shoulder, looking relieved. He was going to have his hands full with Carol, Jenny knew, and she was relieved too, not wanting to be there to watch whatever unpleasantness occurred. When Señora Consuelo got out, Jenny followed her, pausing a moment to look in the car window at her father.

"Don't be too angry with Carol," she pleaded. "She wants terribly to sing. How can you be sure it's right to stop her?"

For a moment she thought her father was going to be exasperated again, but he reached over to pat her hand.

"We'll see," he said.

She watched, feeling completely helpless, while he drove away. But Señora Consuelo was waiting for her, and they went up two stone steps to an open doorway. At the side of the door was a sign that said CIBOLA.

"That was the name the Spaniards gave the mystical Seven Cities of Gold they came searching for," Señora Consuelo said. "Since this is a shop of wonderful riches, it's an appropriate name."

She touched the bell at the door and they stepped into a cool, dim hallway. The house was very old and built of adobe, like most of the others in this area. It looked to Jenny more like a place where people lived than any sort of shop, but she quickly realized that, while someone did live here and use all these handsome pieces, the beautiful furniture was for sale.

In the long living room on their right a woman in a floor-length embroidered skirt and a Mexican blouse, with turquoise earrings dangling from her ears, was talking to a customer. She saw them through the door and excused herself to come running to greet them.

"Consuelo!" she cried. "It's marvelous to see you." She smiled at Jenny as she was introduced, and then waved a hand toward the rear of the shop. "Jim is here and he's waiting for you in the back room."

They walked through a lovely dining room containing an oval table of polished cherry wood and high-backed Spanish chairs of black leather set around it. Señora Consuelo did not pause, but led the way through an arched doorway into a smaller and more cluttered room, which apparently served as office and sitting room for the owners.

A white-haired man, quite tall and thin, rose from an easy chair and came toward Señora Consuelo with his hands outstretched. She began to cry the moment she saw him, and Jim Kingsley held her gently and patted her shoulder. Jenny went quietly to a window and looked out at the yard where there was a shed and a woman working at a pottery wheel.

It was fascinating to watch the clay rise and take shape under the woman's hands, turning almost magically into a graceful bowl. In the room behind her Jim Kingsley and Señora Consuelo were seated on a couch now, talking, and Jenny could not help hearing their words.

"I'm glad you came to town to see me before I left," Mr. Kingsley said. "I've had an emergency here and couldn't get out to the ranch these past weeks. There—you're feeling better now?"

"I'm all right. It's good to feel something again—even pain. I've been numb for too long. Where are you going, and why?"

"I'm flying up to Washington State. There's a trial going on and I want to be there when it ends. Some friends of mine in San Angelo are involved. The

Curtis family. Harry Curtis went to Washington months ago for a fish-in, and he was arrested."

"A fish-in?"

"Yes. He's been away to college, and he made friends with a Tillicut boy who lives in Washington State. His friend's tribe was having their fishing rights taken away, and Harry wanted to help. He's been active in New Mexico too, but he has a principle about Indians standing together, instead of quarreling with each other the way the Hopis and Navahos have been doing lately. Anyway, the Indians went to forbidden territory to fish, the marshals moved in and several of the Indians were arrested— Harry Curtis among them. They believe the rights to fish are legally theirs, granted to them in old treaties the government betrayed, and that they should not be denied. Harry's mother called me last week, and I promised I'd be there for the end of the trial. The Old Ones at the pueblo are taking it hard. Harry's grandfather is a respected medicine man, and I'm afraid he and the others don't understand what Harry has done."

Jenny found herself so interested that she turned from the window in order to watch the two who were speaking.

"Of course they wouldn't understand," Señora Consuelo said. "It's always the group, not the individual, that matters with the Pueblos. One acts for the good of one's own people and always consults with the Old Ones in order to act. They don't admire individual initiative."

"Harry is like a lot of other young Indians these days. He's pulled in several ways. He doesn't want to be exactly like the white man, yet some of the white man's ways have rubbed off on him in college. He wants to see Zuñi ways preserved, and yet he rebels against some of the strictures. Perhaps he'll emerge as a leader, a good one, if he's given a chance."

"Won't that be hard after a prison sentence?"

"You sound like his family, Consuelo. Let's give this trial a chance before we take it for granted that he'll go to prison. The Old Ones won't want outside notice taken of their troubles—though Harry's mother had permission to call me. In a sense I'm one of them. But enough of all that. It's you I want to talk about. What are your plans?"

"I haven't any. Just to live from day to day. There's nothing to plan for."

"You know that isn't true. It's not what Paul would want. When I get back, may I come out to see you? A number of us in Santa Fe want to plan a suitable memorial for Paul. Perhaps an Indian scholarship of some sort."

She answered him sadly. "Come to see me, of course. We'll talk."

"I will. I'm sorry I have to go now, but I'm getting a lift to my plane in Albuquerque. I'm so happy you came to town at last, Consuelo."

Señora Consuelo made a graceful gesture toward Jenny. "This young lady startled me back to life and caused me to come. You can thank her."

"Then I do," Mr. Kingsley said, and his bright blue eyes regarded Jenny warmly. He might not understand what Consuelo Eliot meant, but he accepted her words, and his smile thanked Jenny.

When he had gone, Señora Consuelo sat where she

was, quiet and thoughtful, looking as though she might weep again.

Jenny took a step toward her. "Have you ever been up on top of the mesa?" she asked. "Haunted Mesa, I mean?"

The woman looked at her across the room, her dark eyes brimming with tears she was trying to blink back. "Of course I have. Many times. Paul did a little digging around the kiva up there some years ago, and I helped him."

"Is the climb to the top very difficult?"

"Not when you know the way. But you must never try to go up there alone."

In a rush Jenny found herself putting her idea into words that came out a little breathlessly.

"Greg Frost and I—he's the boy at the Center— have been wanting to climb the mesa. Could you take us up there?"

The tears were conquered, and Señora Consuelo looked at Jenny with new interest. "Why, yes—I suppose I could. Though if you wait until next weekend, there will probably be an organized hike up the mesa for all the conference members who want to make the climb."

"I'd rather go up with just us," Jenny said.

"Then you shall. How about early tomorrow afternoon? There's some work I need to get started on in the morning. Some papers I have to get off."

"That would be wonderful," Jenny said.

They would have to include Greg, of course, she thought. But with Señora Consuelo along, he couldn't do anything to the Indian boy if they should find him.

6. Meeting in the Arroyo

On the way back to Haunted Mesa Ranch, Dad and Señora Consuelo sat in front and talked, while Jenny and Carol sat in back. Carol seemed as calm and unruffled as ever, and Jenny knew she had won.

"Is there going to be a concert?" Jenny asked.

"Of course. Dad can see it will be to my advantage."

Jenny glanced at her sister sitting so straight and assured beside her, the long blond strands over her shoulders looking as though they had just been brushed. "Unruffled" was the word for Carol.

"How can you be so sure of everything?" Jenny asked.

"I know what's right for me—that's all."

"But what if there's a difference between wanting something terribly and really knowing whether it's good for you? You could be wrong."

"Then I'll find out, won't I?" Carol said serenely.

"By that time won't it be too late? You'll be an ignoramus, and educated people will feel sorry for you. You won't be able to talk to them properly. And what if you want to marry a man who has a college education and you haven't?"

Carol turned her head to give her sister her slow, cool smile. "You're sounding like Mom, Jenny-Penny. That's where you heard all those things you're saying."

"Of course. But that doesn't mean they're wrong." Jenny puckered her brows, puzzling. "What if you had a daughter like you—what would you do with her?"

"I'd let her do what she wanted most to do," Carol said.

Her sister, Jenny thought, had a one-track mind and didn't have a whole lot of imagination. She wasn't really thinking about a daughter of her own.

"What if I suddenly announced that I wasn't going to school anymore because I had a wonderful talent and I had to spend all my time on that?"

"But you haven't any wonderful talent, Jenny-Penny," Carol said, not meaning to be unkind.

Jenny subsided. Maybe if someone was as dumb as Carol sometimes seemed, a college education might not do her much good.

After that, neither had much to say. As the miles flew past, Jenny could hear a little of the conversation from the front seat. A snatch now and then told her that Dad and Señora Consuelo were talking about ecology in terms of what Haunted Mesa Ranch had been able to do for the countryside. Apparently land had been donated by the Eliots years before to a Chicano cooperative group for a self-development project, and there had been an animal husbandry program that the Eliots had started. In this arid country it was necessary to take great care of the land and not let it become exhausted, not let the nutrients in the soil be lost. All this was familiar to Jenny, from listening to her father.

After a time, she ceased to hear the voices. Beside her, Carol was humming softly, and Jenny knew she was running over the songs she might sing at the concert. Determinedly, Jenny shut out the murmur of tunes and gave herself over to her own thoughts.

She had succeeded in one plan. Tomorrow afternoon Señora Consuelo would take her and Greg up the mesa, and if the Indian boy was there, he wouldn't be able to hide from them on that great, bare summit. The problem now was whether or not she ought to tell Señora Consuelo about him before they made the climb. As Paul Eliot's wife, she knew a lot about Indians, and she would know what to do. Nevertheless, Jenny felt reluctant to tell her until she had tried another plan she had begun to think about. Perhaps there was a way in which she could meet the boy herself and talk to him before anyone did anything. If she could find out why he was up there, then she would have something definite to tell Señora Consuelo. The plan could be tried tomorrow morning right after breakfast. She would slip away from Greg and do this by herself.

By the time the car reached Haunted Mesa, she was feeling pleased with her own progress.

Dad drove Señora Consuelo to her house, and she invited them all to come in. But Dad shook his head, thanking her, and Jenny knew that all he wanted was to get Carol back to her mother, who would be waiting anxiously to know what had happened.

"Another time I'd enjoy a visit," Dad said.

"Good. Then you must bring your wife with you.

In the meantime let me keep Jenny for a little while. I know it's nearly suppertime, but I have something for her."

Dad agreed, and Jenny was eager to enter the adobe house again. She realized that after being with others for a time, Señora Consuelo might not want to be alone. Perhaps all the unhappy thoughts that waited for her here would come crowding back as soon as everyone was gone.

Inside, Maria came running to greet them. She seemed to accept Jenny now, perhaps realizing that it was good for Señora Consuelo to be in touch with the outside world again. But she was also excited about something.

"A bad thing happens," she began, the moment they were in the living room. "This afternoon I take a siesta. For only a little time, Señora. But when I am asleep there is a thief. Look! I have not touched. Come and look!"

She led the way to the bookcase along one wall and pointed dramatically to a shelf with a row of doll-like Indian figures Jenny had noticed before. Now there was a gap in the row, and instead of an Indian doll, a piece of juniper branch had been placed in the gap.

Señora Consuelo stood before the shelf, examining the row of dolls carefully. "You're right, Maria. One of my Zuñi kachinas is missing. And what is this that has been left in its place?"

She picked up the bit of wood and turned it about in her hands. With a sinking feeling, Jenny saw that the wood had been crudely carved in the shape of a snake.

"Let's look carefully for the doll," Señora Consuelo said. "It may have been misplaced."

Maria shook her head. "No, Señora. Yesterday I dust here. The kachina is in this place. Now is gone."

"It's very strange," Señora Consuelo said. "We never lock our doors here, and nothing has ever been taken. The people who work at the ranch are trustworthy, and we never have any trouble with conference visitors."

"Some small child maybe takes the doll," Maria said.

Señora Consuelo looked at Jenny. "Are there any small children at the Center just now?"

"None that I've seen," Jenny told her. "There's that boy—Greg Frost. He's about my age. But he wouldn't take anything of yours."

Now was the time to tell her about the Indian boy, but if he had stolen something valuable, he would be in real trouble, so once more Jenny held back. There was something mysterious about all this. She wanted to try her plan first.

"What will you do about the doll's being missing?" she asked.

"Nothing for the moment. I want to make sure it hasn't been mislaid before I say anything about it. In any case, missing possessions don't seem very important to me right now. Let it go, Maria." Then, as Maria went out of the room, she held out the piece of juniper wood to Jenny. "This is very curious indeed. It looks as though it has been carved by hand—roughly in the shape of a snake. In Zuñi lore the serpent is related to lightning—the zigzag line. They put that on their hunting arrows too. Yet it's also related to man, and perhaps the serpent stands between man and the lightning and lends him its power. You can see the small forked tongue in the mouth."

Jenny had seen such a tongue before, and she felt uneasy about not letting Señora Consuelo know. But she did not want to talk about the boy until she was sure it was the right thing to do.

"Have you ever seen kachinas before?" Señora Consuelo asked.

Jenny stared at the row of dolls, not looking at the bit of wood that had been replaced on the shelf. "No, I haven't."

"In pueblo ceremonials men dress themselves in costumes like these the dolls are wearing, sometimes with big wooden masks on their heads trimmed with feathers and fur and often with horns attached. They represent the spirits of ancestors or of plants or animals or birds, and they are called kachinas. The ceremonies are very ancient, but the making of these dolls is more recent. A century or so ago the men began to make such dolls to give the children as gifts during the kachina ceremonies. The dolls are copies of the adult kachinas, but they are only toys—they aren't sacred beings. Now they are made to sell to tourists and they can be very elaborate and beautiful. I would like to give you one of mine, Jenny."

Delighted, yet feeling a little shy, Jenny took the wooden kachina into her hands. The square mask on its head was blue, with sticks extending from it, and tiny eyeholes. It wore an animal skin about its waist, with a tail in back, and in its hands it carried forked sticks that Señora Consuelo said were meant to be deer antlers.

"That is Yamuhakto—the kachina that has authority over the forests and over the deer and other animals in the forests. Indians believe that we are all part of nature and we must all respect nature. Only man has been guilty of upsetting the perfect balance of the universe. Perhaps that's what your father is teaching, Jenny. Ecology is concerned with the ways in which man must stop upsetting the balance that the Indians have always respected. Indians have killed animals for food, but they haven't destroyed herds down to the last one. They've burned wood for their fires, but they haven't leveled the forests."

Jenny stared at the blue mask on the doll's head and thought of that gigantic blue head she had seen rising from the edge of the mesa. But why would the boy have a real kachina mask up there, if that's what it was, and why would he want one of these dolls so much that he had taken it from Señora Consuelo's collection?

She repeated the name of the doll aloud: "Yamuhakto. It's a beautiful kachina," she said. "I will keep it always. Thank you very much."

Señora Consuelo rested her hand lightly on Jenny's shoulder. "Thank you for walking into my garden yesterday. Now I think you'd better hurry over to the Center, since it's nearly suppertime, and you must be hungry after our long trip. Will you tell your father again how grateful I am for the lift to Santa Fe? The trip has done me good."

Jenny nodded and went outside to walk toward Juniper. But her gaze, as she followed the road, was on the high rim of the mesa, already darkening as the sun dipped toward the far side. The great shadow of the mountain was creeping across the land, though the sky was still bright.

Everything was serene in the cottage when Jenny walked in. Mother's head was better and she was up talking to Carol, already planning what her daughter was to wear for the concert. Dad had gone off to confer with one of his students, and Jenny slipped into the room she shared with her sister, glad to have it to herself for a little while. She placed Yamuhakto on the bureau and put the roadrunner beside it, finding that they looked well together, even though the roadrunner didn't belong to the forest.

Her thoughts were still confused as to what was best to do. Taking the lunch box from Greg's room was one thing, and not very serious. But taking a valuable kachina doll from Señora Consuelo's collection was something else. She decided that she would not tell Greg about this. Not yet. Her plan for tomorrow morning still had to be tried.

At supper that night there was a little excitement. One of the girls behind the cafeteria table said that some food had been taken from the kitchen that afternoon and the cook was upset. So it was still going on, and sooner or later she and Greg would have to speak out.

Greg and his parents had driven to Taos that afternoon and were not back for supper, so Jenny was not able to tell him that Señora Consuelo had promised to take them up the mesa the following afternoon. She spent most of the evening in the cottage, reading a book from the Center library, and she went to bed early because she was so anxious for morning to come.

When daylight crept in the window, she was up earlier than usual, and she dressed quietly so as not to disturb Carol or her parents. As soon as the dining hall was open for breakfast, she left a note on the bed that she was awake and hungry and would see everyone later. Then she hurried over to the dining hall.

There was no particular problem about getting a few sandwiches put into a lunch packet, and when she had finished breakfast, she left before the rest of her family came in. Nor did she see Greg, which was just as well. By the time she had climbed the small mesa back of the conference buildings, the early-morning sun was turning the great rocky face beyond into a sheet of gold, erasing its streaks of rust-red and deep shadow. It looked powerful and awesome as it rose into the clear turquoise sky. Jenny found that her heart was thumping harder than usual as she went past the open-air conference room and climbed down into the arroyo.

It was eerie down there, and she did not much like the idea of being alone. But she knew her uneasiness was pure imagination and the mountain had no power in its own right. It was big enough to squash her, but it wasn't going to. It had stood there for millions of years and would probably be there millions of years after she was gone. She was too unimportant to attract its attention. Whatever was happening up on top was human, and it had to do with a boy no older than herself. She certainly ought to be able to deal with him. Especially since she had come bearing a gift.

The square lunch box felt bulky under her arm and she was conscious of it every minute. When she saw the boy—if she did see him—she would have to act fast before he could run away again. But by coming here early, perhaps she would be at the foot of the trail by the time he appeared.

The dry bed of the arroyo began to climb toward the mesa and she scrambled up the bank to stand where she could see a great crack in the rock that was the beginning of the way up the mountain. A juniper bush offered a little shade and some concealment. She crouched down in the dusty earth, glad of jeans which protected her legs.

For an endlessly long time nothing happened. Sometimes she could hear birds chirping down in the arroyo, and once a rock slid down the mountain of its own accord, startling her as it bounced through the loose scree at the bottom and rolled into the canyon. Because of the clear air and the great open vault of the sky, sounds traveled a long way, and she could even hear voices from the Center now and then. But no one came down the trail and she began to feel terribly cramped in her crouching position. Was all this effort foolish? The boy might not come for hours—if he came at all.

When her muscles began to ache too badly, she set down the box and stood up to stretch and dust reddish earth from her jeans. She was just trying to find a more comfortable hiding place, when new sounds reached her. Someone was coming down the mountain. He was coming swiftly, half running, and she had the sudden fear that he would be past her and away before she could step out and speak to him. She snatched up the box and stepped around the juniper bush just as he came into view.

It was the same boy she had seen before in the window of the cottage. This morning his long black hair was braided into a pigtail at the nape of his neck, and a twisted kerchief had been tied around his forehead. He slid to a stop at the sight of her, and she burst into hurried words.

"I've brought you some food. See! I've brought you a lunch box from the Center. Don't run away. I don't mean you any harm."

7. Disaster at the Museum

For an instant Jenny thought the boy was going to take flight in spite of her words. His feet in their worn sneakers looked poised for running, and his dark face had the alert look of an animal surprised.

"Please," she said. "Don't run away."

He seemed to relax a little, but he made no move toward her, and there was still that alertness of suspicion in the very pose of his body in jeans and zippered jacket.

"What do you want?" he said grudgingly. He spoke like any other American boy—without accent.

She took a careful step toward him. "I know you took that lunch box from my friend Greg's room, and I think you took it because you were hungry. But you can't go on stealing food, you know. The cook at the dining hall is upset because you must have gone in there yesterday. Pretty soon they'll start looking for you. Greg and I haven't said anything yet, and neither has Señora Consuelo. You took the kachina doll from her house, didn't you?"

Clearly he wasn't going to answer any of this. He came closer and held out his hands for the box. But she didn't want to give it to him right away. If she did, he would simply run off with it up the mountain, and she would know no more about him than before. She held the box close to her chest so he couldn't snatch it, and stared straight into the bright dark eyes that watched her so alertly.

"Have you done something wrong that makes you hide on the mountain? Perhaps the poeple at the Center could help you. Perhaps—"

He broke in, shaking his head. "I am Zuñi," he said.

She sensed the pride in his statement and could guess what he meant. He was a Zuñi and he had done nothing he considered wrong.

"Then why are you hiding up on the mesa?"

He looked at her watchfully and made no answer.

"I'm Jenny Hanford," she said. "Will you tell me your name?"

At least to him Hanford meant nothing, and he answered her, though still grudgingly. "I'm Charlie Curtis."

"Are you from San Angelo?"

But he wouldn't tell her that. "If you want to give me the box, give it to me. I don't want to talk."

"Can't you just tell me why you were going to take my roadrunner from the cottage?"

This time he answered. "I wasn't going to take it. I was only looking at the carving. And I gave it back."

There was nothing else to do but give him the box. He didn't even seem interested in finding out why she had brought him food. He would accept what he needed, and that was all. She put the box into his hands, but before he could turn and start back up the trail, Greg dashed out of the arroyo and flung himself furiously upon the Indian boy. The box went flying and the two boys rolled in the dusty earth. But Greg was bigger and in a moment he was on top, pinning the other boy down, shouting at him angrily.

"You came into my room and stole my lunch! You've been taking food from the dining hall, and now I'm going to turn you in. We don't want any thieves around here!"

He was sitting astraddle Charlie Curtis, who had ceased to struggle and was lying on his back. His dark eyes were fixed on Greg's face, but he said nothing. Greg began to shake him roughly.

"You'd better start talking! Come on! Who are you? Why are you hiding up on the mesa?"

"How can he talk when you're choking him?" Jenny demanded.

She was growing angry now herself. Greg had spoiled everything. She leaned over and gave him a sudden push from the side. He wasn't expecting it, and for an instant he was thrown off-balance so that he released his hold on the boy. In that instant Charlie rolled himself into a wire ball of resistance, squirmed out of Greg's grasp and was off up the mountain, free and running like a deer. Greg recovered his balance, sprang to his feet and started after him. But before he had gone six steps, Jenny was at his back, her fingers hooked into his leather belt, pulling him to a halt. He tried to shake her off, but she closed her eyes and hung on. He gave up abruptly and stood glaring at her.

"What did you do that for? If you'd let me alone, I'd have taken him down to the Center."

"Like a phony policeman on television?" Jenny demanded. "Maybe that isn't what he needs. I just wanted to talk to him first."

Greg stared up the trail where a small dust cloud made by running feet was drifting away. "He's gone now. But I could have caught him again."

Jenny shook her head. "He can run faster than you. And I hope you never catch him. I don't see why you had to come along and spoil everything."

She walked over to the dented lunch box and picked it up regretfully. "I brought him this, and I got to talk to him a little. He even told me his name and said he was a Zuñi. Then you had to come along like a—a—" She was too angry to find a good word.

"Like a phony policeman on television," Greg said, and she saw that he was over his anger and grinning at her. "You sure do get mad," he added.

She was not over her indignation, and his grin made her all the more angry. She held out the lunch box, shaking it at him.

"I brought him this because I knew he was hungry. And then you had to scare him off, so he never got it. Now it may be ages before he comes down again."

"He can't be all that hungry," Greg said. "He took that lunch box of mine, and he's also stolen food from the dining hall. I'd say he's doing all right so far. But he can't keep on. He's got to come down and face whatever it is he's afraid of. He must have done something pretty bad to make him run away and hide. Maybe I'll climb the mesa right now, while he's scared, and then I can—"

"No!" Jenny put a hand on Greg's arm, holding on tight in case he tried to dash away from her. "You know you can't go up there alone. You promised your mother. And besides, it isn't necessary. Señora Consuelo is going to take us both up there this afternoon. At least she was. But I don't know if I want to go up with you now. I didn't think you were such a mean boy, Greg."

He stared his surprise. "You mean Mrs. Eliot has really said she would take us up the mesa?"

"I don't think I'll go," Jenny repeated. "And I'll ask her not to take you."

"You won't do that," Greg said. "You know you want to go up there as much as I do. If we all go up, we'll be sure to find him."

Jenny turned her back and walked a little way up the trail. At the place where it slipped between two high walls of rock, she set the lunch box on a rock ledge where it would be clearly seen by anyone coming down. It was the best she could do. Perhaps Charlie Curtis would come down again later when he was sure no one was around, and he would find it. Unless some animal found it first.

Charlie Curtis. She said the name over again in her mind, forgetting about Greg. Hadn't she heard a name like that just yesterday? When she had been at that place on Canyon Road in Santa Fe, hadn't Mr. Kingsley mentioned the name Curtis?

She walked past Greg, climbing down into the arroyo and up the other side, hardly aware that he had

come with her. It hadn't been *Charlie* Curtis. The
name had been *Harry* Curtis—a Zuñi from San Angelo, Mr. Kingsley had said. An Indian who had
been arrested for helping others to break some law
up in Washington State and was being tried for what
he had done. She wondered if Charlie was a relative
of Harry's. But even if he was, there seemed to be no
connection between Harry's trial and Charlie's hiding out on top of Haunted Mesa.

"Hey," Greg said, when they were out of the arroyo and nearing the little hill that dropped down to
the Conference Center. "Pay attention to me. Didn't
you hear anything I said?"

"I don't want to hear anything you say after what
you did just now," Jenny told him.

"Oh, come off it! You're the one who wrecked everything. If you hadn't pushed me and let that boy
get away—"

But Jenny had heard enough. Once more she
turned her back on Greg and walked rapidly off, and
this time he did not try to follow. She couldn't stand
listening to him right now. She had liked him when
they first met, but now she didn't. He was a trouble-
maker with a chip on his shoulder. She wanted to
have as little to do with him as possible.

He called after her as she walked away. "I'll meet
you outside Mrs. Eliot's house right after lunch.
Okay?"

She did not answer and he didn't call after her
again. Jenny was deep in her own thoughts, turning
over in her mind what she must do. Because it was
necessary now to talk to Señora Consuelo before they
went up the mesa. She must be told about Charlie

Curtis. She would know better than either Greg or Jenny what should be done, and she was more involved than anyone else because of the kachina doll.

Without conscious effort, her feet chose their own way, and she found herself before the turquoise-blue gate of the adobe house. She would be interrupting work, Jenny knew, but this was something that ought to be done before Señora Consuelo went blindly up the mesa this afternoon, not dreaming of what was going on.

Maria met her at the open door, but this time Jenny was made welcome and ushered into the long, cool living room, where she stood looking at the painting of Haunted Mesa. She could hear Maria talking in another room, and in a moment Señora Consuelo came through the door.

Today she wore a dress of saffron yellow, with a turquoise belt. In spite of her smile, the sadness was in her eyes again.

"Hello, Jenny," she said. "Maria tells me you have something important to talk to me about."

"I'm sorry to interrupt," Jenny said. "I know you have work to do—"

"Yes—papers that should have been gone through long before this. However, I've made a good start and I can take a break for a little while. What has happened, Jenny?"

She blurted it out quickly, before she could hesitate and fail to say what she had come here to say.

"I think I know who took your kachina doll. I think it was taken by a Zuñi boy who is hiding up on top of the mesa."

"Well!" Señora Consuelo voiced her surprise. "You

have been playing the detective! Come and sit down, Jenny, and tell me all about it."

They sat together on the long, moss-green sofa, and Jenny told her what little she knew—about the moment when she had seen something move on top of the mesa, about the curious figure with the enormous blue head, about the Indian boy who had taken her roadrunner, only to throw it back, and about the theft of Greg's lunch box. And then about what had just happened at the foot of the trail that led up the mesa.

"He said his name was Charlie Curtis," Jenny finished. "Perhaps I'd have found out more if Greg hadn't come along and spoiled everything."

"Curtis," Señora Consuelo repeated thoughtfully.

"Yes. Isn't that the name Mr. Kingsley mentioned yesterday?"

"I believe it was. Of course there could be many Curtises, interrelated, if this boy is also from San Angelo. It's too bad I can't reach Jim now to talk to him about this. Since he's well acquainted there, he might know what to do. I think you were right to move cautiously, Jenny. We may turn this over to the authorities at the Center eventually, but perhaps we need to give this boy more of a chance to explain first. We don't know what he has done, or what this is all about, and there is a totally different culture operating here."

Jenny waited, not altogether understanding what she meant.

"Too often," Señora Consuelo went on, "the Anglo American expects everyone else to live according to his rules. He sets values and concepts that may be totally different from those of the Spanish American, or the Indian American. That's why I'd like to know a little more about Charlie Curtis before we begin to treat him according to our rules."

Jenny released a long sigh of relief. "I suppose that's why I haven't said anything about this before—even to you. I was afraid someone might just rush in and arrest that boy—or do something else to hurt him. But of course he shouldn't have taken your kachina doll. The food doesn't matter so much, but the doll was something valuable."

"Nevertheless, he left the snake carving in its place. I'm not sure just what that means, but I do think it indicates that he isn't simply stealing. He's trying to make some sort of return for taking something he needs."

"Needs?" Jenny said.

"Perhaps. Food, of course. That's easy to understand. And he must be getting water somewhere too, because there isn't any up on the mesa. But the kachina is something else. And so is that great blue head you saw up there. It sounds like one of the kachina masks from a Zuñi ceremony. But of course we don't have the key that would cause any of this to make sense to us. Perhaps we can find that key if we go up there this afternoon."

"Will you talk to Greg before we go?" Jenny pleaded. "So he won't do anything foolish again."

Señora Consuelo smiled. "I'll try. And don't worry anymore, Jenny. We'll work this out without hurting anyone if we can. I'll expect you both here right after lunch. Say one o'clock or so. And wear good hiking shoes."

She came to the door with Jenny and waved as she went off.

Jenny returned to Juniper and told her mother that Señora Consuelo was going to take her and Greg on a hike up the mesa that afternoon.

"That's lovely," Mother said. "And very generous of Mrs. Eliot. I wonder if she would mind if you took Carol along?"

Carol was modeling one of the Western outfits she had brought with her to the ranch and would probably wear for the concert. It was a lime-green silk shirt with a yellow kerchief tied at the neck, and well-cut green pants. A silver concho belt that she had bought in Santa Fe was buckled around her waist and she looked very trim and beautiful. But the idea of climbing the mesa didn't appeal to her.

"Jenny can have it. All that hot sun and a dusty climb. No, thanks—not unless I can go up on a burro."

"I don't think that's possible," Jenny said, feeling relieved. Carol's presence would have put a whole new element into the adventure ahead of them, and she didn't want to cope with that too.

"Anyway," Mother said, "you needn't try on any more clothes, Carol. That outfit is fine, and if you want to make a change partway through, you can add your gray suede jacket with the fringe. Get out of those good clothes, now, and we'll all go out and do something. I've seen very little of this place since I've been here."

"Do what?" Carol asked, untying the kerchief from her neck.

"I understand there is a remarkable museum here at the ranch. We can go and visit it before lunch."

Carol did not look entranced over the thought of visiting a museum, but since she was getting her way on the important things, she smiled amiably and went into the next room to change her clothes. Jenny was glad to have an interesting way to spend some time until one o'clock, when she could return to Señora Consuelo's.

It was only a short drive along a dirt road to the museum, and when Mother had parked the car, they got out and walked toward the long, low adobe building with the flags of the United States and New Mexico flying above it. Everything looked quiet and undisturbed in the bright sunlight. When the three visitors stepped inside onto the tiled floors it was pleasantly cool.

On each side of the long main room were glass cases, and Jenny walked to one that displayed the small skeleton of a very old dinosaur. The sign said that these small dinosaurs had come before the big ones, and that several findings had been made in the area around Haunted Mesa. But even as she read the sign, Jenny became aware that all was not so quiet as might be expected in a museum.

From around a bend of the hall that led into another wing came the sound of voices—rather excited voices. Mother and Carol looked in the same direction, and Jenny went ahead to see what was happening around the corner.

Two men, a boy of about seventeen, and a woman were standing before one of the display cases, and they all looked as though something had them thoroughly upset. The boy was sweeping up broken glass from the floor, and behind the little group Jenny could see the jaggedly broken window of a display case.

"We've never had any vandalism here before," the woman was saying. "But you can see—that stone was thrown through the glass sometime between when we closed last night and opened this morning."

The case with the broken window held various Indian objects, and Jenny moved closer, leaving Mother and Carol standing at the turn in the hallway. She stared at the things in the case, some of which were sprinkled with broken glass. Laid out on a piece of deer hide in the display were the contents of a Navaho "singer's" medicine bundle. Reading the card of explanation, Jenny could see a fur collar with a reed whistle attached, several clumps of feathers, a necklace of beads, some shells, and four crooked snakes carved from wood. All these things apparently had different uses and meanings.

Jenny's breath caught at sight of the snakes, and she edged nearer to see them better. The two men and the woman paid no attention to her, though the boy sweeping glass gave her a suspicious look. She could see quickly enough that these Navaho snakes weren't like the cruder carvings that Charlie Curtis must have made. In another part of the case were several masks, drums, and other objects.

"Look here," the woman was saying, holding something out for the two men to see. "I found this near the stone that smashed through the glass."

She was holding out a twisted piece of juniper wood. Jenny didn't need a second glance to know that it too was a carved snake, but not so carefully finished as those on display. Feeling somehow guilty, she moved away from the group and went to look at another display. But she could still hear the three talking behind her.

"Is anything missing?" one of the men asked.

"Yes—a Zuñi drum. That seems to be the only thing, though I haven't had time yet to make a complete inventory."

"If I may use your phone, Mrs. Brewster," the man said, "I'll call the State Police. This is such an unlikely thing to have happen out here that we must get after it at once."

Feeling a little sick, Jenny stood with her back to the grownups, so they couldn't see her face. Now Charlie Curtis had taken something important from a museum, and he had done serious damage besides. Once more he had left one of those carved snakes— almost as if it were his signature. Now the police were to be called in, and it was all getting out of hand. She wondered what would happen if she should step up to one of these people and announce that she knew who had taken the drum and where he was hiding. But she could not do that without talking to Señora Consuelo first. And that must wait until one o'clock.

When Mother and Carol walked through the rest of the museum and then went outside to see some of the live desert animals that had been collected here,

Jenny went along. She looked at everything, but very little registered. The only thing that seemed important to her now was the ticking of an imaginary clock in her mind. A clock whose hands moved slowly—all too slowly—on toward the hour of one. Then she could be rid of her worry and her guilt. She could place this new disaster in the hands of someone who would know what to do about it. Until then, she must just hold on.

Back at the cottage, Jenny stood outside for a little while, her gaze fixed upon the mesa. But nothing moved on top of that great red mass, and somehow she was glad. Perhaps Charlie had gone away by now. Perhaps they would never find him. But why—why in the world would he steal a drum?

Was it because she was thinking of a drum that she seemed to hear an odd, distant thumping that traveled faintly through the sunny air?

Behind her, Greg spoke. "Do you hear it, Jenny?"

She didn't turn around and she could not answer.

"It sounds like a drum," Greg went on. "Charlie must have a drum up there and he's banging on it."

"No," Jenny said softly. "That's not a real drum. Don't you know the story? There are spirit drums that sound sometimes on top of Haunted Mesa. Drums played by the ghosts of the Indians who died there."

Greg paid no attention to such nonsense. "I wonder how Charlie ever got a drum up there?"

So Greg hadn't heard as yet about the theft from the museum. Jenny did not enlighten him. But even after she went inside the cottage, she could hear the echo of that strange rhythm running through her head. Up on top of the mesa a modern Indian boy was beating a drum to the old, old gods.

No one else seemed to hear. No one came out of another cottage or from any of the buildings to look curiously up at the mesa. Only she and Greg had heard. Jenny put her hands over her ears, but she could not stop the rhythm that pounded in her head.

8. Up the Mesa

The climb up Haunted Mesa was just about as Carol had said it would be—hot and dusty. At least Señora Consuelo knew the way without hesitation, and they climbed steadily, talking very little.

There had been time for discussion earlier. Jenny had gone to the adobe house ahead of Greg, and she had blurted out the news about what had happened at the museum. Señora Consuelo had listened soberly, and Jenny knew she was troubled.

"This isn't something we can keep to ourselves any longer," she said. "The police will have to be told what we know."

"Right away?" Jenny asked.

Señora Consuelo thought about that. "Perhaps it won't make any difference if we wait a little while. Say until after our climb up the mesa."

Jenny smiled at her, enormously relieved. If Charlie had committed burglaries, of course the police would have to be told. Yet at the same time she kept having the feeling that something unusual was operating here. As though some power stronger than Charlie was causing him to do these things, and that if they only understood what that power was, then his acts would be explained and perhaps forgiven.

Señora Consuelo was watching her. "It's a curious thing that's happening, isn't it, Jenny? I have never seen this boy, and you haven't seen him long enough to get to know anything about him. Yet we're both somehow concerned and involved in trying to protect and help him. I'm not usually on the side of lawbreakers. The rest of us have to be protected, even when we feel that the lawbreaker needs help. But this time we seem to have our sympathies strongly involved. With very little reason. I wonder why."

"Maybe it's because of—of the snakes," Jenny said hesitantly.

"The snakes?" Señora Consuelo went to the shelf where the carving of a serpent still rested between two kachina dolls. When she turned around she had the bit of wood in her hand. "Perhaps you're right. If he was just stealing, why would he leave this sort of mark behind him? It must mean something, though I'm not sure what. Anyway, Jenny, let's see if we can find him and talk to him this afternoon. Then we'll know better what we must do."

When Greg came, she spoke to him about approaching the Indian boy with care and not doing anything to frighten him off. At least Greg seemed to listen to what she said, though Jenny was never sure what unexpected thing he might do.

When they started up the mesa they climbed first into the great crack between high rock walls where Jenny had left the lunch box. At least the box was gone, and there were no traces around to indicate that an animal had found it. There were few snakes in this area, Señora Consuelo said, but they should not put hand or foot on a rock ledge without looking first.

After a steep climb, the rough trail wound into the open behind the mesa. Here the aspect of the mountain was very different from the other side. Instead of steep ramparts of rock that could never be scaled, the earth sloped most of the way down, crumbling into loose scree near the foot. But their climb up the crack had put them above this loose stone, and partway up there were juniper bushes clinging wherever they could find a foothold in the earth. Their roots held the soil together and made it possible for climbers to pass among them on the way to the top. Luckily there were no dangerous precipices on this side, though there were still some ramparts of rock near the top, and Jenny wondered what the climber would do up there.

Halfway up the mountain they paused to rest. From this side of the mesa the Center buildings could not be seen, and there was nothing in view except more rocky outcroppings and dusty land studded with juniper and sagebrush. In the far distance, as always, there were mountains.

"It's a good thing Haunted Mesa isn't a real mountain," Señora Consuelo said, "even though we call it that. It looks vast and high because it rises straight up from the ground below. But the elevation isn't really too great when you climb it."

Greg was eager to go on. Neither Jenny nor Señora Consuelo had told him about the drum stolen from the museum, but his eagerness to meet the boy he had come to regard as an enemy drove him. In spite of Señora Consuelo, there still might be trouble up there, Jenny thought, if Greg started to get tough again. And it would be all the worse when he heard about the drum.

Perhaps Señora Consuelo sensed this, because she would not allow herself to be hurried. While they rested and drank lemonade she had brought in a thermos, she talked a little about the Zuñis. Through all the centuries of interference from the white man, they had clung to their own ways and preserved their own culture and religion. Most Pueblo Indians were Catholics, but they had never given up their own beliefs and they still celebrated them in colorful ceremonies.

"Have you heard anything more about that Zuñi boy who was arrested?" Jenny asked.

"Only that the trial should end anytime now," Señora Consuelo said. "That was in the paper. It must be very hard for the Old Ones at San Angelo. They won't understand his going off to support the cause of Indians so far away. I'm sure this isn't something his own pueblo would have approved. In the past no member of a group stepped out to do something on his own without the entire pueblo behind him. What was done was always for the good of all."

"My dad says maybe it's a good thing that white men have been helping the Indian manage his affairs," Greg said.

Señora Consuelo answered him quietly. "The Indian managed his own affairs very well for centuries before the white man came. We've done our best to weaken him and make him dependent. But we haven't wholly succeeded, thank goodness. Something of his spirit has survived, and it's coming to life in the young. Now even the government in Washington is beginning to see that the Indian must have self-determination. Like every other American, the Indian must have a chance to be what he wants to be. He needs help because we've made him poor in many cases. We've tried that awful thing called 'termination'—which means that we've tried to erase everything Indian about him. But we haven't succeeded. The young Indian today doesn't want to be an American Indian—someone set aside. He wants to be an Indian American in his own right. There's a difference. You can be an American and still have your own heritage."

"Can't we get started again?" Greg asked impatiently.

Señora Consuelo stood up. "Of course. We're rested now. But, Greg, go a little easy, will you? I mean don't judge too quickly, no matter what we find up there."

Greg mumbled under his breath as he started ahead, but Jenny felt that they couldn't count on what he might do.

The trail was clear now until it reached the top, where it disappeared between craggy cliffs, and Señora Consuelo took the lead once more. Near the very top, Jenny discovered that steps had been carved into the stone. Here the rock was protected from the weather, so that the ancient, worn steps remained. Jenny could imagine Indians mounting them—those who had fled up here from the Spaniards and whose ghosts haunted the top of the mesa.

When Señora Consuelo reached the summit she

climbed out onto a ledge of rock, then held out her hand to pull Jenny up beside her. Greg managed by himself, and all three were on top of the mesa.

Jenny had never been in a place like this—at the very top of the world. The wide, level plain of the mesa stretched out before her, rough with patches of earth and broken rocks, clumps of juniper—and otherwise a great emptiness. If she had expected, somehow, that Charlie Curtis would be immediately visible when they climbed up there, she was disappointed. No living thing stirred, and only the scraggly juniper trembled in the breeze. In every direction lay the empty plain, dropping off on all sides like the end of the world, and a great wind was blowing across the mountain.

She moved away from the other two, walking to a place where she could look down upon the arroyo at the foot of the mesa and at the cluster of conference buildings, which had shrunk in size, so that they looked tiny. It was hard to believe that those buildings down there were real, so dwarfed were they by the height of the mesa. It was hard to believe that she had stood among them.

Señora Consuelo moved to Jenny's side, while Greg went poking around disgustedly. Probably he too had expected Charlie to be quickly seen, once they reached the top.

"There's no place to hide up here," he said.

Jenny paid no attention. From here, the world was too big to be realized all at once. Perhaps this was the way the astronauts felt when they found themselves leaving the earth—with all of it stretched like a map below them and the great blue vault of the sky overhead.

Señora Consuelo pointed toward a distant horizon. "We can see the Rio Grande now—over where the greenery winds. You can always tell a stream in this country because that's where you'll find the trees and shrubbery growing thick."

Looking where she pointed, Jenny could see towns clustered in the dusty land and follow winding roads with her eyes. That was Taos in one direction, and the road to Santa Fe in the other. The great range of mountains, some of which still had snow on the highest peaks, was the Sangre de Cristos, the very foot of the Rockies.

"The Spaniards called them by that name," Señora Consuelo said. "It means the 'Blood of Christ,' because the snow shines red in the setting sun. You can still see it sometimes, just as it was in the days of the Conquistadores."

It was all breathtaking, and it made Jenny feel so small and unimportant that she had no thoughts for anything else for the moment. But Greg was moving around on top of the mesa and he called to them.

"What's this over here? It looks as though someone started to build a house."

"It *was* a house at one time," Señora Consuelo said as they walked toward him. "The Indians who sheltered up here built one of their ceremonial meetinghouses they call a kiva. You're looking at its ruins, Greg. It was part of a circle of houses at one time. Long before they fled up here to defend themselves from the Spaniards, they knew they might need this place. So while they still lived in the pueblo below, they carried the materials up here to build their houses—the adobe bricks and the wood. There was even a little earth where they could raise some crops. Water must have been the biggest problem, because it rains so seldom here. But they managed somehow. They could hold off the Spaniards from reaching them up here, but the Indians sometimes made raids down to their camps and took what they needed before they fled back to the top of the mesa."

The ruins were now no more than an earthen circle, with an entrance marked by a break in the crumbling adobe, and the long room of the kiva indicated. Jenny thought of the people who had lived here, struggling desperately for the freedom they loved. They had been a peaceful people and they had never wanted to fight. For how long had the rim of this mesa been the edge of the world for them? As it had recently become the edge for Charlie Curtis?

Jenny wandered away by herself and found a flat rock she could stand upon. There she turned slowly in her own small circle, facing first one point of the compass and then another. At each turn she let her gaze travel over the surface of the mesa, searching for any possible hiding place. Mostly the ground ran level till it dropped off into space. In only one place did several pinnacles of rock rise to break the line that was the edge of the mesa. But their steep sides offered no hiding place, any more than did the flat plain that led to them.

"I'm afraid our quarry may have gone," Señora Consuelo said. "But we won't give up yet."

She had spent little time looking over the mesa top, once it was evident that no one was in sight. At this height the stunted junipers were too low to offer hiding places, and the kiva ruins came scarcely as high as one's ankle. But she was walking among those ruins now, with a faraway look on her face. Perhaps she was remembering the times she had come here with her husband, when he had been digging in this very place to unearth more of history.

Suddenly she bent over and picked up something from the earth. "How very strange," she said.

Greg ran over to her and Jenny followed. On the palm of her hand rested a curious little animal formed out of stone. It had a head, a short, thick tail, and four legs, barely indicated in the black stone. Thongs had been wrapped about the body, and blue beads and something that looked like an arrowhead were thrust beneath strands on the creature's back.

Señora Consuelo's eyes were rapt as she gazed upon the small object in her hand, and she began to speak musingly, as though she remembered words.

"Black bear, thou art stout of heart, but not strong of will. Therefore I make thee the younger brother of the Mountain Lion, the guardian and master of the West, for thy coat is the color of the land of night."

The words were beautiful, mysterious.

After a moment Señora Consuelo explained. "The Zuñis believe that in the beginning all men belonged to one family. The father of the sacred bands lived in the City of the Mists, at the center of the world. He was guarded on all sides by his six warriors. These were the prey gods, the animals. The black bear guarded the West, where the night begins."

"But what is that?" Greg asked, staring at the object in her hand.

"It is a Zuñi fetish. Every Zuñi man likes to have his own fetish. In the days when he hunted, he believed that the qualities of the animal he chose would become his. The fetish was a sort of mediator for him between the man and the animal-god. There is a great deal of ritual connected with these fetishes, and each man's fetish is precious and private to him."

"Could this fetish belong to Charlie Curtis?" Greg asked.

"I doubt that, because he's very young. Though he may have brought it here with him. Why, I can't guess. No Zuñi would take another man's fetish. Unless the man were dead."

Greg was growing restless. "Anyway, what do we do now? If Charlie is gone, how do we find him?"

"I'm not completely sure that he is gone," Señora Consuelo said. "There is one more place to look."

Jenny gazed around her once more. "But if he's here, where is that big blue mask I saw the other day? And where is the drum he was beating?"

Señora Consuelo sighed. "He has probably hidden them."

"Hidden them?" Greg cried. "But where? There's no place to hide anything up here."

"My husband wrote a chapter about Haunted Mesa in one of his books. And he explored it thoroughly first. I was with him when he found the caves."

Jenny's heart gave a sudden bump of excitement, though she wasn't sure whether she was glad or sorry. Somehow she had hoped there might be a confrontation with Charlie Curtis up here, so that the boy could talk to Señora Consuelo. Perhaps he would have trusted her. On the other hand, she was a little relieved to find him gone. Because then, if information about him was turned over to the police, he would be away where they couldn't catch him. Of course if he took the drum from the museum with him— She shut her eyes, wincing at her own thoughts. She continued to be confused and uncertain about what she ought to feel and think.

Greg Frost felt no confusion at all. "Where are the caves? Let's get going!"

"We can't go into them," Señora Consuelo said. "They are dangerous. The hollowed sandstone has crumbled in places. My husband went down on a rope, but I didn't go into them at all. They begin where those pinnacles of rock rise, at the far end of the mesa."

Greg would have started in that direction at once, but Señora Consuelo's hand was upon his arm firmly, holding him back.

"No, Greg. You will come with me, and you will do only what I allow you to do. You and Jenny are in my charge now, and I'm not going to have anything happen to you."

She did not hurry on the way, and Greg had to control his impatience. She carried the bear fetish in her hand as she walked, and she had begun to talk in a strangely loud voice. Jenny wondered if she was talking for Charlie's benefit—in case he could hear her. Perhaps warning him that they were approaching. So he could make a choice?

On the way she told them more about fetishes and about how precious one like this would be to the owner. A fetish must never be lost. It was usually kept in a special, woven container and there were rites to be performed involving it.

"This arrowhead," she tapped the back of the bear, "stands for the Knife of War. It's supposed to protect the wearer from the enemy if he attacks from unexpected quarters. Perhaps it would even protect the hunter from an attack by a real bear. The hunter who carried this fetish would assume the strength and courage of the bear."

Greg was scarcely interested. All his attention had focused upon those needles of rock ahead. As they drew closer, Jenny could see that the splinters rose sharply from a solid base, but she could see nothing in the way of an opening into what looked like sheer rock. Señora Consuelo slipped the small black bear into a pocket of her slacks and stood still for a moment, staring ahead at those rocky spires.

Jenny felt her flesh crawl as she paused beside her. She had the curious feeling that someone was watching them. The sensation of eyes upon her—eyes that stared with anger and resentment—was strong. She wondered if Señora Consuelo felt this, too, and if that was why she hesitated. But though the woman's gaze was upon that clump of rock they had neared, there was no telling what she might be thinking.

Greg had stopped beside them, and now he dropped to one knee. As Jenny watched him, she caught a flash of light from something on the ground.

"Look!" Greg cried.

When Jenny bent over him, she saw that a wooden-handled knife lay on the ground, with a partly carved twist of juniper branch beside it.

So there was no longer any doubt. Charlie Curtis had been carving those serpents. He had been doing it up here.

"Leave the knife there," Señora Consuelo said firmly when Greg would have picked it up, and he obeyed reluctantly.

Once more, she began to walk toward the spears of rock, and Jenny and Greg moved with her, one on each side. Greg was more eager than ever now—too eager—and again Señora Consuelo's hand was on his arm, restraining him. Jenny felt only a great uneasiness and perhaps a rising sense of fear, though she was not sure what it was she feared. It was as though something besides Charlie Curtis might be hiding in those caves.

The afternoon sun beat down upon the top of the mesa, but the wind blew steadily across its surface, so that the air was cool. Nothing at all moved around the spires of rock, or anywhere else. Only the three of them seemed alive on the great mountain-top.

"Where is the opening to the caves?" Greg asked, speaking softly, as though he did not want whoever hid there to know he was near.

Señora Consuelo did not drop her voice. "The opening is masked. You can't see it from here, any more than you can see the way out at the bottom. Escape is possible down there, though very dangerous."

When they were only a few feet from the rock, she stopped with a hand on each one's arm. Now the spires of rock looked more massive and formidable, less dwarfed by the expanse of the mesa. Jenny could feel the pressure of tense fingers upon her arm. Señora Consuelo was uneasy too.

"Wait here," she said. "Both of you."

She walked toward the sheer face of reddish rock at the base of the spires until she could touch it if she put out her hand. And now she spoke to the rock.

"Are you there? Are you down below in the caves? If you are, Charlie Curtis, please come up. It's necessary for us to speak together. We are your friends."

Nothing at all happened for several moments. Then a curious sound arose from the depth of the rock—a wild wailing that had in it all human grief, all sorrow for humanity. It was the wailing of a lost spirit, and Jenny clutched Greg, shivering. She could tell that he was frightened too by that awful sound, and he made no effort to step closer to the rock. Señora Consuelo stood her ground. When the wailing died eerily away, echoing against other mesas all around, she raised her voice and spoke to the invisible opening.

"There's no use trying to frighten us. If there are spirits of the mountain here, they won't harm us. Come out, please, and talk with us, Charlie Curtis. It's necessary to talk, because soon the police will be looking for you."

The rock stood impassive in the bright sunlight. And then, suddenly, there was movement against its surface. Where there had been nothing, a hand had emerged from a slit in the rock, followed by a head and a body. Charlie Curtis raised himself from behind the concealing barrier and stepped out before them onto the mesa top. He neither smiled nor scowled, but his eyes were the eyes of a very frightened boy.

Señora Consuelo spoke to him gently. "I am Consuelo Eliot—Paul Eliot's wife. My husband was a friend of your people."

Charlie nodded briefly. "I know you. I have seen you with your husband in San Angelo."

"Then it should be possible for you to trust us a little, Charlie. It should be possible for you to tell us what trouble you are in and why you have come here to Haunted Mesa."

"No," he said. "I can't tell you."

She went on as gently as before. "I know your people, Charlie. The Zuñis have great honor and pride. So I know there is some strong reason behind what you have done since you've come here. The taking of food we understand. But when a doll is missing from my kachina collection, when a drum is removed from the museum and a glass case smashed—this becomes serious. If you can tell us the reason, perhaps we may be able to intercede to help you."

The boy regarded her impassively without answering.

"A Zuñi is not a thief," he said.

The fear was still in his eyes, but he lifted his chin in a gesture of pride. "Nothing has been stolen," he said. "I have left my promise."

"You mean the serpent carvings?"

He bowed his head mutely.

"But you must understand that these carvings

don't have the value of the things you have taken. They don't pay for the replacement of glass."

"There wasn't time to make good carvings," Charlie said. "I can do better."

Señora Consuelo sighed, and Jenny remembered what she had said about differing cultures. Even Consuelo Eliot, with her understanding of Indians, was not able to establish understanding now, because what had meaning for her had no meaning for this boy.

He seemed to sense this, for a slight smile touched his mouth—almost as if he sought to reassure her.

"Nothing has been stolen," he repeated.

She gave up and chose another direction. "Charlie, is the Harry Curtis who is on trial now in Washington State a relative of yours?"

The hint of a smile vanished. "He is my brother," the boy said. "My brother does what is right—but he will go to prison. White men will send him there."

"You can't be sure of that. The trial is ending now. A good friend of mine and yours—Jim Kingsley—has gone to see if he can help your brother. Your people in San Angelo have asked him to go."

"My brother will go to prison," Charlie repeated.

"Does your family in San Angelo know where you are?"

The boy returned her look without expression, and Jenny knew he would not answer.

"Perhaps," Señora Consuelo went on gently, "it would be best for me to go to the pueblo and talk with your family."

"No!" The sound was explosive, with a strange mingling of fear and anger. "No—you must not go!"

"So they don't know where you are? Isn't it possible, Charlie, for you to tell me why you are here?"

But Charlie did not mean to talk, and it was as if an invisible wall of misunderstanding had fallen between them. Not even Señora Consuelo knew how to breech it.

There was a long moment in which no one spoke, but Charlie Curtis began to edge back toward the caves, and Jenny knew he would disappear into them in another moment.

Señora Consuelo reached into her pocket and drew out the bear fetish. "I found this lying on the ground on the mesa," she said. "Is it yours?"

The boy regarded the small stone shape in her hand as though something about it frightened him. Then he reached out and snatched it from her. In a moment he would be gone, fleeing into his cave, and he would not come out again. Jenny spoke hurriedly.

"Were the juniper snakes left as—as hostages, sort of? I mean, are they meant to show that what has been taken will be returned?"

The boy turned to her almost eagerly. "That's right! My brother can talk very well. When he speaks, everyone listens. But I can't talk like that. You have said what I mean."

Señora Consuelo gave Jenny a quick, pleased look that warmed her. "But if this is true, Charlie," she said, "can you tell us when these things will be returned?"

He shook his head. "There must be a Shalako first."

"A Shalako! But that won't be held until November or December. It's a winter ceremony. It takes forty-nine days and involves many people. It will be held in Zuñi, and all your people will go there. What has that to do with these missing objects, or your hiding on top of the mesa?"

"The Shalako will be here," the boy said. "On the mesa at night."

"But that's impossible." Señora Consuelo was losing patience. "Many, many people take part in that ceremony, and all the countryside knows about it ahead of time. Houses must be visited and blessed. There could be no Shalako up here. And even if it were possible, you couldn't wait here until winter."

"Winter comes soon," Charlie said enigmatically. "Maybe in a few days."

Señora Consuelo was beginning to look at the boy in a troubled way. Greg, with less sensitivity, spoke aloud.

"He's crazy," Greg said.

There was anger in the Indian boy's face, but he did not move or look at Greg. "I am not crazy," he said. "When white men don't understand, they call others crazy."

"Perhaps that's true," Señora Consuelo said. "But you have to understand our viewpoint too. When the police start looking for a drum and a kachina doll, they won't be very polite about it. And they will be dealing with facts, Charlie."

"But not with the truth," Charlie said.

"What do you expect us to do?"

"You can go away. I didn't ask you to climb the mesa. I asked for no help. There is danger if you come here."

"Oh, Charlie! What danger?"

"The Pueblos were here before the Apaches or Navahos. Our Old Ones come from them. Their blood is mine too. Some of our people died here long ago. Maybe they watch over this place. They don't want you here."

Señora Consuelo glanced at Jenny and Greg. "Perhaps we'd better go now. But you'll have to come down soon, Charlie. And when you do, remember that we are your friends."

The expression he wore shut them all out. He had no belief that they were his friends. He turned away and started toward the spears of rock that hid the entrance to the caves.

"Wait," Señora Consuelo said. "If there is any danger up here, it's in the caves. You must know that. My husband went down by a rope one time and he said the walls were not safe. Something could happen to you in there and no one would know."

Charlie paid no attention. He had nearly reached the wall of rock when the strange wailing sound rose again from deep within the caves. It moaned on a high, shrill note, then sank and died away, while the echoes went on wailing.

A look of terror had come over the boy's face. "Go away!" he cried. "Go away—go now!"

The urgency of his appeal was so great that not even Señora Consuelo could withstand it. She caught Jenny and Greg by the arm and hurried them off across the top of the mesa.

Even Greg looked scared. "What was that?" he asked.

Señora Consuelo did not speak until they were halfway back to the place where the trail descended. Then she paused and they all turned to look once more toward the caves. There was no one in sight. Charlie had disappeared, and nothing but the wind-stirred junipers moved on top of the mesa. There was no other sound but the wind.

"What was it?" Greg repeated.

"I'm not sure," Señora Consuelo said. "I thought it was Charlie the first time we heard it. Perhaps it's some trick of the wind down those old, hollow pipes in the rock."

The breeze seemed colder now and Jenny shivered. "Let's go down," she said.

No one wanted to stay, and for a few moments they were well occupied climbing down the steep, worn steps that dropped between the walls of rock until they were in the open again at the back of the mesa.

Here the going was easy enough, and Jenny spoke for the first time since they had left the top.

"What is a Shalako?" she asked.

Señora Consuelo was willing enough to explain. "It's an important ceremony the Zuñis hold. It has many aspects, but there is a final dancing that begins after midnight on the last day. Among other things, the Shalako is a prayer for rain and for the well-being, the health of the people. It's very complicated, and certain houses are chosen for the celebration."

"Then of course it couldn't be held up there," Greg said.

Señora Consuelo answered quickly. "No, of course not." But Jenny heard an unexpected note of doubt in her voice.

After that no one had much to say until the long climb down was over. By the time they came out above the arroyo, the sun was low in the sky.

"What are we going to do?" Jenny asked Señora Consuelo.

Greg answered before she could. "We have to go to the police. There isn't anything else to do. You didn't tell me about a drum being taken. That boy up there is bananas. He's got to be stopped."

Señora Consuelo moved more slowly as they reached the road to the Center. "I'm not sure about that, Greg. Perhaps he's disturbed and confused. I'm sure he needs some sort of help. There's something here we don't understand. Perhaps we should wait a little while longer."

Greg scowled. "How long?"

"Don't try to be so tough," Señora Consuelo told him. "Perhaps this is the time for a little patience and kindness. Until things come clear."

"But how long?" Greg repeated.

Señora Consuelo turned toward the mesa and looked up at the vast mass of rock they had just climbed. A mass that had already turned to black shadow, with the sun behind it.

"Perhaps until after the Shalako," she said.

9. Masked Intruder

It was hard for Jenny to talk to Carol and her parents about the climb up the mesa. Since she could not tell them yet what had really happened, she could only describe the marvelous view, the kiva ruins, the sense of ancient history she had felt on top of the mesa. She hoped that Greg was being equally careful. Señora Consuelo had told him not to be tough, and she had a feeling that he had not liked that. Jenny hoped he might want to prove that he was more generous than she thought.

While they were at dinner that night something surprising happened. Maria came from Señora Consuelo with a note for Mrs. Hanford. Mother read it and smiled as she handed it to Jenny.

"Mrs. Eliot is inviting you to come to her house tonight as an overnight guest. You're to have your own room and have breakfast there in the morning. Would you like to go?"

Jenny read the note with pleasure. "Oh, yes—if it's all right with you."

"You seem to have made a hit," Dad said, and Jenny was aware of Carol's puzzled look. She realized suddenly that she hadn't been thinking about Carol very much lately. She had had too many affairs of her own to think about.

After dinner she returned to the cottage to pack a few things in a canvas flight bag for the night, kissed her parents, and started off for the adobe house. She had gone only a little way on the road when Greg fell in beside her.

"Where are you going?" he asked.

When she explained, he looked unexpectedly envious.

"Mrs. Eliot's pretty great," he said. "She's somebody I'd like for a friend."

"Then you won't do anything right away about Charlie?"

He shook his head. "I guess I'm not so mad at him anymore. I don't know what's going on, but maybe she's right that we ought to wait. Mrs. Eliot won't let things get out of hand, and in this case maybe it isn't the police we need after all. Just so the museum gets back its drum."

Jenny smiled at him, liking him the way she had that first night when they had met at the campfire. He seemed to be two boys sometimes. One was real, and one was something rather fierce that he made up when he was playacting to get attention.

"I'll walk you to Mrs. Eliot's house," he said.

They didn't talk much on the way, but the silence was comfortable. There were just three people who knew about Charlie up there on the mesa, and Greg was one of them.

At the blue gate he hesitated. "Maybe tomorrow I'll take another box of food up to the trail," he told her.

"That would be great," Jenny said and went inside.

The evening was cool and a fire of piñon logs had been lighted in the adobe fireplace, giving the room a fragrant scent. Señora Consuelo looked beautiful in a long gown of turquoise blue, and blue sandals on her slim feet.

"Do you notice the scent of piñon?" she asked. "That's a smell that will always mean New Mexico to me. Come, Jenny, and I'll show you your room."

It was a small room just off the big living area, with an Indian rug on the floor and a colorful Indian blanket woven in a design of yellow and gray on the bed. Besides the bed, the room was furnished with a small desk and chair, a bookcase, and a handsome painting on the wall.

Jenny dropped her bag on the floor and went to stand before the picture of Indians circling in a dance. Some had skins tied around their waists, some were barefooted, others wore leggings and blue moccasins, and all had fanciful masks on their heads—some quite large and eerie-looking.

"An Indian artist painted that," Señora Consuelo said. "The figures are of masked kachinas. That is one of the Zuñi ceremonies of the Shalako."

Jenny nodded as she studied the picture. "It must have been a blue mask I saw that time up on the mesa—but a very big one."

"I wish I could understand," Señora Consuelo said. "There's such a big piece missing to this puzzle. If we had it, perhaps everything would come clear."

"Charlie was scared when we were up there," Jenny said.

"Yes, I think he was. I believe he was afraid we might discover something he wanted to keep secret. When that wailing started, he was terrified. Yet he wasn't afraid to go back to the caves. Well, it's no use puzzling about it tonight. I think something is going to happen up on the mesa, and perhaps then we'll know."

"I hope Charlie won't get arrested," Jenny said.

"We'll try to prevent that. But of course that will depend on what he does next. If the thefts continue, we'll have to tell the people at the Center. I hope you'll be comfortable here tonight, Jenny. I'm happy to have you as my guest. It was kind of your parents to let you come."

"But of course they'd let me!" Jenny exclaimed. "I *wanted* to come."

Señora Consuelo smiled as she led the way back to the living room, and Jenny found that two chairs had been drawn before the corner fireplace, a reading lamp beside each. Señora Consuelo chose the green one with a high winged back, and motioned Jenny toward the other. A book lay on the seat and Jenny picked it up as she sat down.

"That's one of my husband's books," Señora Consuelo said. "Perhaps you'd like to dip into it tonight. When he was alive, we often used to sit here like this, sometimes reading, sometimes stopping to talk or read aloud some passage we found in a book."

Jenny knew she was blinking back the tears, and she opened the book quickly to look at some of the pictures and give her hostess time to recover.

"I found I didn't want to sit here alone tonight," Señora Consuelo said. "And you and I have some experiences in common by this time that make us special friends."

Jenny nodded, pleased. "I just saw Greg, and he isn't going to say anything about Charlie being up on the mesa."

"That's good," Señora Consuelo said.

After that they sat in silence for a while, each reading her own book. Now and then they talked. Once about Carol's plans for a concert at the beautiful Santa Fe Opera House that had been built on the outskirts of town. This time Jenny found she didn't mind talking about her sister.

"Perhaps Carol's right," she mused. "Perhaps this is too big an opportunity for her to pass up."

"I wonder what her life will be like," Señora Consuelo said, her eyes on the snapping crimson flames in the fireplace. "I hope she doesn't come to feel that she's alive only when people are applauding her and giving her their adulation. Because that can be only a small part of really living."

"That's what Dad keeps telling her, but I don't think she listens. She loves being famous and popular."

"The center of the world. We all have a little of that desire in us. Some more so than others. But the real satisfactions come when we reach out to other people and learn what they want. That's what I must do now, young Jenny. Grief can be selfish. I've let it become the center of the world for me, and that's wrong too."

The thoughtful silence that followed was broken when Maria brought in a tray with cups of steaming hot chocolate and the honey-ginger cookies Señora

Consuelo had promised. The chocolate was made in the Mexican way, beaten frothy and with a hint of cinnamon.

The evening couldn't have been nicer, Jenny was thinking. Quiet, without excitement, but with a feeling of friendship between two people who had found they were not entirely separated by the years between.

It was nearly bedtime when the telephone shrilled and Señora Consuelo went across the room to answer it. Jenny heard the catch of her breath as she listened to someone at the other end. Her face seemed to light with pleasure and she nodded to Jenny across the room.

"That's marvelous, Jim," she said. "I couldn't be happier. So now you'll be bringing Harry home?"

Jenny could hear a murmur of words from the other end of the line.

"In that case, you'll fly home tomorrow afternoon? . . . Good. Jim, will you do me a favor? I know Harry will be anxious to get home to San Angelo, but we need him here at Haunted Mesa first."

Again there was the murmur on the line.

"No, Jim—you must listen to me. Not San Angelo first. Bring him here. His young brother Charlie is in trouble. I can't explain—it's too long a story for the phone. But perhaps Harry can help if you will bring him to my house. You can phone San Angelo that he'll be a day late, but don't say anything about Charlie. Will you do that, Jim? . . . You're a dear. This really is important. You'll drive out from Santa Fe? . . . I'll see you tomorrow then."

She hung up the phone and returned to her chair, her face alight with excitement.

"You heard that, Jenny? The judge has acquitted every one of those Indians—Harry among them. A few years ago that might not have happened. But this time there was real justice. So he'll be coming home."

"Perhaps we ought to go up on the mesa tomorrow and let Charlie know?"

Señora Consuelo thought about that for a moment. "No—I'd rather not. I want to wait until Harry can go with us. Then we'll go up again. Because we don't really know what is happening up there, or whether it even concerns Harry. But Harry will know best how to deal with his brother and whatever trouble he's in."

This was good news, and Jenny was anxious to tell Greg what was going to happen. But that too would have to wait until tomorrow.

The two before the fire talked for a little while longer and then Señora Consuelo announced that she was one for an early bedtime, so perhaps they could turn in.

A plate of cookies accompanied Jenny to her room. When she was ready for bed and had crawled beneath the Indian blanket, she found her head whirling with so many thoughts that she was afraid she would lie awake for a long time. But she had taken that strenuous hike up Haunted Mesa, so while she lay in her warm bed, with moonlight streaming in a window and touching the strange masks of the Shalako dancers, she fell fast asleep.

Moonlight moved slowly away from the picture

and across the white wall in its progress through the night. It lighted the small bookcase, which Jenny had decided she must examine tomorrow morning, and vanished from the room as the moon moved across the sky. The great mesa was quiet under the moon's radiance. Only on the trail down the mountain did something stir, flitting swiftly on light feet. The cottages and buildings of the Center slept, the horses and burrows were quiet at the corral. Only that single, stealthy figure moved in the night, finding its way among the buildings, following the dusty road that led to the adobe house.

Perhaps the visitor had been this way before, since he knew of the weak catch on one window, and he moved without a sound to open it and climb inside. In the big room there was darkness, which did not trouble him, but certain chairs had been moved, so the pattern was changed, and he did not discover this at once. Without difficulty, he found his way to the row of kachina dolls and felt along the shelf. Then, having accomplished his purpose, he retreated toward the window. It was Jenny's chair drawn before the fireplace that blocked his way when he took a different path across the room. When he ran into it, the creaking sound caused the visitor to kneel in the shadows, tensely waiting and alert.

In her room with its door ajar, Jenny stirred and wakened. There had been a sound. Whether in her dreams or real, she wasn't sure, but she had a strange sense of waiting silence in the next room. Señora Consuelo's bedroom was farther away, and Maria was at the back of the house. Charlie! Jenny thought. What if Charlie had returned?

Moving quietly, she slipped out of bed and into slippers, pulled on her robe. All remained quiet in the next room, and from the doorway she could see nothing but shadows and the moonlight against the windows.

"Charlie?" she whispered. "Charlie, is that you?"

Nothing answered, but a room with someone in it had a different feeling from a room that was empty, and she sensed an intruder crouching in the shadows.

"You can come out," she said, still keeping her voice low as she moved into the room. She had no fear of Charlie Curtis.

The rush of movement took her by surprise. A hand thrust her roughly out of the way, so that she went sprawling on one of the Indian rugs. By the time she could regain her feet and run to the window, the figure was rushing away in the moonlight, and she could just make out that it was wearing a huge mask.

For the first time real fear overcame her and she shouted for Señora Consuelo.

In a moment her hostess hurried from her bedroom, clasping her silk gown about her, her silver-streaked hair in a long braid down her back. Behind her came Maria, uttering small cries of alarm. Lights flashed on in the living room and Señora Consuelo went to put her arms about Jenny.

"You're trembling, dear. What is it? What happened?"

Jenny found it hard to speak. She waved her hand toward the open window and struggled for words.

"There was—someone here. He—he pushed me away and went out the window."

Maria ran to the window to look outside, but Señora Consuelo turned to the shelf of kachina dolls and stood searching it with her eyes. "Another one is gone," she said.

Maria uttered exclamations of distress and talked angrily of calling the police. Her mistress stood in silence for a moment, staring at the new space on the shelf. Then she turned to quiet Maria.

"Tomorrow we will decide what to do. Go back to bed, Maria. I think there will be no more disturbance tonight."

While Maria went off reluctantly, Señora Consuelo closed the window and examined the latch. "This must be fixed if we're going to have trouble. Was it Charlie again, Jenny? Did you see him?"

"I saw a figure, but it was wearing a mask. I heard a noise and I thought Charlie might have come back. So I came here and called to him. But it was too dark to see clearly, and I think the figure was too tall for Charlie. He had that big blue mask on his head. I could see that when I looked out the window."

"Oh, dear!" Señora Consuelo dropped wearily into a chair. "If there is someone else involved—a grown person, perhaps, that changes everything. It makes it even less innocent."

Jenny found that her heart was thumping raggedly in reaction to what had happened. The hand that had thrust her out of the way had been rough, and she was still frightened.

"I think we'd better go to bed and put all thinking off until morning, Jenny. Decisions made in the middle of the night when we're anxious are seldom well thought out. Will you be afraid in your room?"

Jenny wasn't sure, but she didn't want to cause more worry. "I'll be all right."

Señora Consuelo came with her to her room and tucked her into bed, dropped a light kiss on her cheek.

"I'm sorry this had to happen," she said. "I didn't mean my hospitality to turn out like this. But I really think everything will be quiet now. Whoever it was got what he wanted—"

Once more Jenny settled down in bed, pulling the covers to her ears against the chill. The moon had disappeared behind clouds and the night outside was quiet except for a rising wind. But now it was hard to sleep, and Jenny drowsed off and on, sometimes dreaming snatches that she couldn't remember when she wakened, only to drop into dreams again.

But one thing was not a dream. It must have been long after midnight when she wakened to hear that distant sound. Like someone beating a drum. Perhaps on top of Haunted Mesa. The sound added to the sense of deep mystery. Toward morning she fell asleep, and the rest of the household slept too, after their nighttime excitement, so it was Jenny who arose first.

When she was dressed she went into the empty living room to look around. There was the gap on the shelf of kachinas—where two dolls were now missing. The carved snake was still there, but no second snake had joined it.

Remembering the drum she had heard in the night, she went to the door and opened it to look up at the mesa. Then she stared in astonishment at the red tile doorstep.

Someone had placed two kachina dolls upon the step, and beside them lay a small wooden object. She bent and picked it up. It was a tiny deer carved from light brown wood. The carving wasn't something recently done, because it had been polished by much handling. The animal was seated on a small block of wood, its delicate legs curled under it, and its head turned over one shoulder. Its ears were pricked alertly and two slender horns rose between them as the long, beautiful animal face looked peacefully at the world.

This must have been something that Charlie had made sometime ago and that he had carried with him, treasuring it. But he had left it here on the doorstep with the dolls. What did it mean?

She went back inside to find that Señora Consuelo was up, dressed in gray slacks and a white shirt, her hair once more combed into a soft roll at the back of her neck.

"Good morning, Jenny," she said. "I hope you got some sleep after all our excitement. And I hope you're as hungry as I am. It's a wonderful thing to be hungry, Jenny. I don't think I have been for a long while."

"Señora Consuelo—" Jenny began, but her hostess went on, not giving her time to speak.

"I've been thinking while I showered and dressed this morning, and I believe we mustn't wait any longer. What happened last night is too serious. If there is someone else—perhaps a grown man—involved besides Charlie Curtis, then we must not postpone going to the police."

"Please," Jenny said. "Please come and look."

She led the way to the door and the woman stood beside her, staring down at the doorstep in sudden silence. Then she picked up the two dolls.

"Yes, these are mine. Someone has returned them."

"And this too." Jenny held out her hand with the small carving on the palm.

Señora Consuelo took it from her and examined it with delight. "It's an antelope. A lovely piece of carving. Nothing like those crude serpents."

"I think Charlie made it. He said he could do better work when he had time, and you can see it's not new."

"But I don't know what all this means. Why were the dolls taken, and why were they returned?"

"Last night I heard a drum on the mesa," Jenny said.

Señora Consuelo carried the two dolls back into the house and restored them to their place on the shelf. Then she handed the carving to Jenny.

"I think you should keep this."

Jenny accepted the carving with pleasure, but she was worried. "What are you going to do now?"

"We're going to have breakfast as soon as Maria can get it for us. And then, Jenny, I think we're going to wait. The returning of the dolls makes a difference. We'll wait until Jim and Harry get here this afternoon. I don't feel competent to deal with this alone."

Jenny relaxed a little, but she had thought of

something else. "I wonder if the drum has been returned to the museum—since someone brought back the dolls."

"A good point," Señora Consuelo said. "I'll phone as soon as the museum is open."

Jenny found she could eat a good breakfast, now, since Señora Consuelo was going to take no immediate action about Charlie Curtis. Jenny still didn't want to go to the police. Not even though the ugly memory of the mask and that rough hand pushing her would haunt her for a long time.

After breakfast, however, the mystery deepened. When Señora Consuelo phoned the museum director, it was only to learn that the drum had not been returned.

10. Harry Curtis

It rains very seldom in New Mexico, but the storms Jenny had heard about are most apt to come in late summer, and when it does rain, there is usually a deluge.

Jenny stood at the window of the Center's main lodge and looked out at the streaming countryside. Black clouds had been sweeping by overhead all morning, sometimes dropping long fingers to earth that were slashed with lightning and released torrents of rain.

Because of the rain, the day had moved slowly, but now at last it was afternoon, and as she stood at the window she thought of Mr. Kingsley and Harry Curtis driving up from Santa Fe in the rain. And she thought of Charlie up on the mesa. But at least he had those caves to crawl into—though Señora Consuelo had said they were dangerous. What she felt mainly was a sense of waiting.

Waiting for the storm to blow over—which it was beginning to do. Waiting for that car from Santa Fe to arrive. Waiting for whatever was going to happen up on the mesa, once it arrived.

A log fire had been built in the lodge fireplace

against the cold and rain, and when she looked over her shoulder, Jenny could see her sister sitting on the couch before it, a picture of disconsolate boredom. For the moment they had the room to themselves. Most people were off at classes, and others had remained in their cottages, out of the wet.

Jenny spoke over her shoulder to Carol. "What's the matter? You don't look a bit happy. But you should, since you got your way about the concert."

Her sister sighed. "It's all so boring. Nothing to do. Even college would be better than this. There'd be other kids at least, and I expect I could get in some singing."

Jenny left her post by the window and went to drop onto the couch beside Carol. "Does that mean you've decided to go?"

"Oh, I suppose I might as well. For a time, anyhow. Mother and Dad will be after me forever if I don't."

Jenny felt a flash of enlightenment. "Did you make a bargain with Dad? Did you promise to go to college if he let you do the opera house concert?"

Carol merely grunted, but Jenny had her answer.

"I think you're doing the smart thing," she told her sister. "I wouldn't miss college for anything."

"But you don't have anything else you want to do," Carol pointed out.

For the first time, Jenny found that she didn't altogether accept this. "Oh, I expect there'll be lots of things I'll want to do."

Carol looked at her, puzzled. "You sound different. I mean different since we came here."

Jenny thought about this. She didn't feel any different. "I don't know what you mean."

"You've stopped being jealous of me," Carol said with unexpected understanding. "You never needed to be, you know. You're clever in lots of ways I'm not. I've just got one thing I can do well. It's the only way I know to make people pay attention to me."

Jenny stared at her in surprise. She hadn't thought Carol had noticed that much.

"Why do you want to make people pay attention to you?"

"Because," Carol said, watching the fire, "—because I'm not anybody by myself. It's only when I'm singing, and they're listening to me and applauding, wanting to hear me—then I'm really somebody."

Almost shyly, Jenny reached out and touched her sister's hand. "That's the silliest thing I ever heard. I've always thought you were terrific."

But Carol was concentrating on her own train of thought. "Maybe I'm a little scared to find out what I'm really like when I don't have a guitar in my hands. Maybe I'd just go back to being that dumb kid I was in grade school."

"Don't be silly," Jenny repeated. "You don't have to have everybody in the world paying attention to you every minute in order to be somebody. Nobody pays any attention to me—" She broke off suddenly because that wasn't true right now. She had made some new friends on her own. She jumped up and returned to the window. "I'm mixed up too. Maybe I've gotten used to having no one notice me until now. I just wonder what it's like to be someone like

Señora Consuelo, who knows what she is. At least she does now that she's getting it all together again."

Carol had returned to watching the fire, lost in her own thoughts, and Jenny looked out at the rain. The lodge window did not look upon the mesa, and she couldn't see its wet, glistening face as she had seen it earlier.

But this morning even Señora Consuelo had lacked confidence. She had admitted that she didn't know how to deal with the mystery of the mesa. At least she hadn't gone to the police, so Charlie Curtis—whatever he was up to—had been granted a little more time. Sometimes it could be dangerous to delay going to the police, but in this instance, Jenny felt Señora Consuelo was right.

The main door to the lodge opened, and Carol turned around hopefully. But it was only Greg who came in. She yawned and went back to watching the fire.

"Hi, Jen," Greg said. "The rain's about stopped, but it's still too wet to go tramping around much. The sun will dry it up fast. But for now I wonder if there are any games in this place we could play."

At the moment Jenny wasn't interested in games. She put a finger to her lips and gestured toward the far end of the big lounge. Greg understood and came with her.

"Any new developments?" he asked.

She told him about staying at the adobe house overnight, and about all that had happened. "Señora Consuelo wants to wait until Mr. Kingsley and Harry Curtis get here before she does anything. She said I could come back to her house when they get here."

Greg looked envious. "Everything happens to you. Do you think she'd care if I came too?"

"We can ask her," Jenny said.

He stood beside her at the window, and they looked out at the wide stretch of land sloping away toward the Rio Grande. You couldn't see nearly so far from here as you could from the top of the mesa, but there was still a lot of land and mesas and mountains out there. Clouds still blew across the sky, but they were moving away toward the east.

"Look—a rainbow!" Jenny cried.

The great bow arched from a rise near the lodge, to lose itself in the valley, its colors blazing sharply for a few moments, gradually fading and dissolving into mist. Beside her, Greg pointed.

"There comes a car along the road to the ranch!"

They watched for a little while as it came straight ahead in their direction.

"It must be Mr. Kingsley's car," Jenny said. "Let's go down to Señora Consuelo's so we can be there when it arrives. Then we can ask her if it's all right for you to stay too."

Jenny left word with Carol as to where she would be and they went off to follow the dirt road. In spite of the rain it was already drying in spots and they could hop over the muddy patches. The dry earth had soaked up the torrent as it fell, and only the shrubbery was still covered with raindrops.

There was no view of the road from the adobe house, and Señora Consuelo was glad to hear of the approaching car. She too thought it must be Jim

Kingsley, and she had no objection to Greg's staying to see what happened. He was as much a part of this as they were.

"I'll be relieved to turn this problem over to someone who may know better how to handle it than I do," she said.

Once more there was a cheerful fire in the big room, though the sun was coming out now and the afternoon would grow warmer.

They could hear the car before it took the turn to the house with the blue gate, and Señora Consuelo went to stand in the doorway, while Greg and Jenny waited at a window. Mr. Kingsley was driving, with a young Indian man in the seat beside him. He pulled the car up in front of the house and both men got out. Jim Kingsley was as tall as Jenny remembered, and rather thin and weather-beaten, with bright blue eyes that focused with a certain intensity on whatever he saw. The young man who followed him toward the door of the house was not so tall, and he was more stockily built. Jenny noted at once that there was a family resemblance to Charlie Curtis in the bright, dark eyes, the wide shape of the face, even in the way he wore a band about his head to hold back his black hair.

It was strange about the faces of differing peoples, Jenny thought. On the streets of New York she had seen many nationalities when she had gone with her parents to the city. They all had the same collection of eyes, noses, ears, mouths, foreheads—but in each case they were put together with subtle differences. It was that way with Charlie Curtis and his brother. You looked at them and you thought "Indian" in your mind. Just as Mother had said that when she was in a foreign country she was always picked out as an American right away. Skin colors helped with some indentifications, of course, but Harry Curtis' skin was only a little darker than her own tan.

When the greetings and introductions were over, Señora Consuelo gathered them around her fire and sent Maria for refreshments.

"I think it's wonderful about the trial, Harry," she said. "Perhaps we're just beginning to understand a lot of things for the first time."

Harry, like Charlie, expressed very little with his face, but he spoke his thoughts more readily.

"It's time somebody understood. Indians have been talking for hundreds of years, but no one really listens. Maybe a few, here and there—like your husband, Mrs. Eliot. Being an Indian, I didn't expect to be let off at this trial."

"Perhaps you were being treated as an American," Mr. Kingsley said quietly.

Harry looked at him gravely, and then turned to Señora Consuelo. "Will you tell me what this is about my brother Charlie being in trouble? Mr. Kingsley said you wanted him to bring me here first."

Maria came in, carrying a tray with a silver coffeepot and glasses of milk for Greg and Jenny. Not until Maria had gone did Señora Consuelo try to explain.

Then she told about articles being taken from the adobe house and the museum, and of the way Greg's lunch box had disappeared. She told of the encounter in Greg's cottage with Charlie Curtis, and about Jenny's meeting with him on the trail.

"So we decided to climb up the mesa and see what we could learn," Señora Consuelo said. "But I'm afrail we learned very little. Your brother is up there, but we don't know why. In every case that something has been taken, he has left a carving in its place. We understand that he means this is a promise that these things will be returned."

As she spoke, Señora Consuelo rose and went to the shelf where the carved snake still rested. She brought it back for Harry to see.

He took it from her and studied it without expression.

"Does the fact that it's a serpent have any significance?" Señora Consuelo asked.

"The Zuñi respects the serpent," Harry said. "But perhaps it's mainly that this twist of juniper branch resembles a snake. It would be an easy carving for my brother to make quickly and roughly. But I don't know why he would leave it here."

"My two kachina dolls have already been returned," Señora Consuelo went on. "But not until Jenny had rather a scare last night. Jenny, will you tell them what happened?"

Jenny told her story as exactly as she could and finished with the finding of the dolls and the antelope carving on Señora Consuelo's doorstep that morning.

Harry nodded thoughtfully. "I know that carving. My brother has talent. I want him to go to the Indian Arts Institute in Santa Fe next year. But it's strange that he would give that carving away."

"I think he did because he felt bad about what was happening," Jenny said.

Harry smiled at her slightly, as though he was grateful for her words.

"Who do you suppose the other man can be, up on the mesa?" Señora Consuelo asked.

"I don't understand any of this." Harry shook his head. "If someone else is with him, I don't know why Charlie would go along with it in the first place."

"He spoke of a Shalako being held very soon on top of the mesa," Señora Consuelo said.

"A Shalako!" Harry sounded unbelieving.

"I know. I pointed out that it was a winter ceremony with many people involved, and he said a very strange thing. He said it would be winter in a few days."

Harry sat quietly for a moment longer, staring at the fire. Then he looked at Señora Consuelo.

"I think I must telephone San Angelo. There's a phone at the pueblo store and the man in charge may know something."

"Of course," Señora Consuelo said. She led the way to an extension in another room and returned, courteously leaving him to talk alone.

Mr. Kingsley told them a little more about the end of the trial and of the jubilance of the Indians in the area. "It was a fair judgment. The Indians were right and they shouldn't have been arrested in the first place. They were peaceful and caused no trouble. Harry's friend was grateful and he wanted Harry to stay a while. But Harry said he must get home to reassure his family. He didn't have the blessing of the Old Ones when he went away, and he has to make his peace with them."

Harry finished his call and joined them again. For a few moments he said nothing at all, lost in his own thoughts. Then he looked at Mr. Kingsley.

"I must go up on the mesa," he said, and Jenny knew he wasn't going to tell them what he had learned on the telephone.

Señora Consuelo asked no questions, and she didn't try to dissuade him. "Then let us go with you. We'll do nothing unless you ask—we'll leave everything to you—but I think you must let us stand by. It's because of Jenny Hanford that your brother hasn't been arrested. She came to me and I have been willing to wait."

Again Harry thought solemnly before he answered. "Okay, Mrs. Eliot. If you want to go. I don't understand what's happening yet. The man at the store couldn't tell me. But he did tell me one thing, and perhaps my brother needs me in this trouble."

"Someone else is on the mesa with him?" Mr. Kingsley asked.

"Yes," Harry said, but he did not tell them who it was.

Señora Consuelo went to a window and looked outside. "I wonder if we should wait until tomorrow? Before we reach the top the sun will set. We would have to come down in the dark."

"Then I will go alone," Harry said.

"Perhaps we needn't wait," Mr. Kingsley told him. "I've been up there at night, and it's not a dangerous climb. There are no steep drop-offs on the far side of the mesa. I have a flashlight in my car that we can take along."

"Is there likely to be any danger to us on the mesa from this other person?" Señora Consuelo asked. "Charlie hasn't been taken as a hostage, has he?"

Harry shook his head. "I don't think there's any danger."

"Good. There'll be a full moon tonight, and I've been up there in the past with Paul when the moon was full. I have more flashlights. For Jenny and Greg this would be an experience to remember always, as long as the risk isn't too great."

Jenny's heart warmed toward her friend. Señora Consuelo hadn't forgotten what it was like to be young and have an opportunity given you for a wonderful adventure. She only hoped her parents would let her go.

"What do you expect will happen up there, Consuelo?" Mr. Kingsley asked.

"I'm not sure," she admitted. "But somehow I think it will be winter tonight when the moon is full."

For the first time Harry smiled. "You have an understanding heart," he said.

So it was decided, Señora Consuelo herself went to talk with Jenny's and Greg's parents. She couldn't explain fully, but she convinced them that the expedition to the mesa on the night of the full moon would be something worth doing. And she was able to convince them that it would be perfectly safe. Both she and Jim Kingsley knew the trail well, and it was an easy climb if one knew it, as Greg and Jenny had found in the daytime.

While the Señora was gone, Maria hastily put together a stack of sandwiches and packed them into two flight bags, which the men would carry. Three more flashlights were found, and jackets and sweaters were collected. The Center director was told by Mr. Kingsley that he was taking a small party to the top, and there were no objections made. This had been done before.

The sun was already dropping behind the mesa by the time they set out. Jenny stayed close to Señora Consuelo, and Greg was right behind. He was no longer trying to be in charge of things, but seemed willing enough to follow.

A torrent of water must have rushed down the arroyo that afternoon, but though there was some dampness, the water was gone and they could cross easily.

When they reached the trail up the mountain, Mr. Kingsley and Harry went on ahead. As Jenny followed, she felt glad to be a part of whatever was going to happen, yet at the same time she was more than a little uneasy. Of all of them, she was the only one who had felt that rough hand pushing her down in the dark living room last night. She couldn't feel as sure that there would be no danger as Harry seemed to be. Yet she knew that if she expressed her worry and persuaded them that the strange man up on the mesa might, after all, be dangerous, she wouldn't be allowed to go.

When the trail wound around to the back of the mesa and they climbed into the open, she gasped with pleasure at the sight of the sun about to set all over again beyond a farther mountain. There were still clouds in the west, after the rain, and the sunset had flamed to a bright crimson that faded out to pale emerald, painting the clouds as it swept up the sky. The distant mountains were touched with pink, and there was a scent of juniper and sage on the air. Somewhere an owl hooted. Jenny stood very still on the slope of the mesa, drinking it all in. Just ahead of her, Señora Consuelo had stopped too, and when she glanced around, Jenny saw the glisten of tears in her eyes.

"A moment like this should always be shared," she said and held out her hand.

Jenny took it shyly, understanding that her friend did not want to remember loneliness at this moment.

When the sun was gone, the sky remained blue and bright for a time. Darkness would not set in until they were near the top of the mesa.

Señora Consuelo called to the men, who had started ahead. "Perhaps we should stop here on this slope and have supper before we go on. It will be easier to eat while there's still light, and we may not want to stop by the time we've made the climb."

The men agreed, so Jenny and Greg helped to unpack the two flight bags that contained picnic things—sandwiches and thermoses of coffee and milk. An outcropping of rock shielded them from the wind, so they could sit on the rough ground and eat in fair comfort. Jenny found herself hoping they would reach the top before the light was completely gone across the eastern land, so that she could see that tremendous view again. Also she had a feeling about the coming of darkness that she did not want to face or admit. Remembering that figure in a huge blue mask, she did not want to meet it again in the dark.

No one ate in a hurry, however, except Harry Curtis. He was drawn to the top as Jenny was, and even though he was careful not to express emotion, Jenny sensed that he was worried and that the phone call he had made to San Angelo had not reassured him.

At last they had finished, and there was only a little climbing left. Everything was packed up and put away into the bags, and the flashlights were distributed, because they might soon be needed. Once more they started up, hurrying a little because the light was fading, and there were still those ramparts ahead where steps led up the crevice between walls of rock. At least there were no precipices that could be dangerous on this climb.

Just as they reached the foot of the ancient steps carved into the rock, a sound from the top of the mesa made them all stop to listen. Jenny held her breath because she knew that sound. Now it thudded much nearer and louder than when she had listened to it in the night.

Up on the mesa someone was once again beating a drum.

11. The Shalako

No one said anything, though they all heard the sound of the drum. Harry started up the steps, and the others fell in behind. By the time Jenny and Greg reached the top, Harry, Mr. Kingsley, and Señora Consuelo were already on the mesa. They all stood in silence, looking down the great flat plain in the direction from which the sound of the drum was coming.

It was hard to see that far, as dusk closed in, and Jenny walked partway across the mesa so she could look out upon the wide view. The moon was already mounting the eastern sky, an enormous yellow globe that would seem to shrink as it reached its zenith overhead. Below the mesa, lights were on in all the buildings and cottages of the Center, like a collection of fireflies glowing in the twilight, and in the distance were other clusters of lights, marking towns.

Down the mesa the drum still thumped, and Harry started in that direction. No one switched on a flashlight as they followed him quietly, without speaking. Their steps were not soundless on the stony ground, however. Though she tried to be careful, Jenny heard loose rocks skitter under her feet.

As they neared the drumming figure, so that he emerged from the dusk, Jenny could tell that he had heard them. He still beat upon the hide cover of the drum, but his head turned toward them watchfully. The drummer was Charlie Curtis.

Strangely, Harry did not hurry ahead now, but put out a warning hand to those behind. "Wait," he said softly. "Go slowly."

"Yes," Señora Consuelo whispered. "Whatever it is—let it happen."

They moved in a close group, slow step by slow step toward something that was unknown. White man's knowledge did them no good now, for this seemed a mesa haunted by history. Only Harry appeared to wait with a greater knowledge than theirs, though even he could not fully understand what was happening. He had moved too far into the white man's world.

As the last daylight left the earth, the full radiance of the moon took over, and the mesa was lighted in a new way. The sun lent color to the world. The moon took it away. Now there were only patches of silver light and jet-black shadow, while overhead a billion stars seemed very close.

Their small group was not far from the caves, when from the shadow-streaked rock there suddenly rose that strange, wailing cry Jenny had heard before. The drum did not lose a beat as the wailing lifted toward the sky and the echoes cried out as if with pain—a sound that was like a weeping for the dead. It was as if it bemoaned the loss of all those who had died in this place hundreds of years before.

The chimney of the caves gave the sound its extra, magnified dimension—eerie and not of this earth.

Then it ceased as suddenly as it had begun, and from the deepest shadow a strange figure appeared. In the moonlight it could be seen that he wore the skins of animals, with a cascade of beads around his neck. On his head he wore a great, high mask that seemed to grimace at them as he moved in the direction of the drum. Charlie's rhythm never faltered, and in the group behind Harry no one moved.

Slowly the figure began his stylized dance—movements that had been handed down over the centuries.

"The Shalako has begun," Consuelo Eliot whispered. "For him it is winter, and he is not alone."

Jenny's skin prickled at the words. She could see what was meant. It was as if that single dancer out there on the mesa top moved in concerted steps with many others. By his gestures and movements he recognized other dancers. In his mind the mesa was peopled as he wound his way toward the ruins of the kiva. Jenny could almost see a hundred people out there—watching, like themselves. Watching those who danced beside the man who wore the mask.

The drumbeat quickened and the feet of the dancer moved faster, his arms raised as though he carried something in each hand. At the broken entrance of the kiva he stopped and seemed to perform some ceremony.

"He's going to bless the house," Jim Kingsley whispered. "He's asking for the health and well-being of the people."

As they watched, the dancer's movements changed.

He raised the tall mask and put it aside. When it lay on the ground at his feet, he began to chant in a high quavery voice—the voice of a very old man. His face was invisible at this distance in the moonlight, but his hair was black and bound with a band across his forehead in the ancient way. The chanting was like nothing Jenny had ever heard. It rose and fell eerily, with words she could not understand and a sound strange to the white man's ears. It went on and on, while the moon crept up the sky, bathing the mesa top with its cold, unearthly light. The boy at the drum was tiring. Sometimes his rhythm faltered, and once the old man turned to regard him sternly, so that Charlie stiffened and picked up the rhythm again.

But at last the dancer himself must have found that his strength was failing. He missed a step and stumbled, then righted himself and went on.

"It's Gray Fox, isn't it?" Mr. Kingsley whispered to Harry.

The Indian nodded. "Yes, it's my grandfather."

"I know him very well," Mr. Kingsley said. "I'll go to him before this becomes too much for him."

"No," Harry said. "You mustn't interrupt."

But Mr. Kingsley had recognized the signals of deep fatigue, and he moved toward the dancer and called out.

At once the old man straightened and faced the little group he had not noticed until now. Then he uttered a loud, vengeful cry, and with all his strength regained, he hurled himself toward them.

Charlie left his drum and called out in alarm. "Run! Run—or he will hurt you!"

Señora Consuelo took Greg and Jenny each by an arm, and drew them with her a little way off on the mesa. Behind them came the sound of struggle, and when they turned, Jenny could see that Mr. Kingsley and Harry were holding the old man, restraining him until his struggling became less. He was muttering now, wildly, and Jenny caught some of the words.

"Spaniards who killed my people! White men who destroy! White men who have put my grandson in prison!"

"No, no, Grandfather," Harry cried, as the old man renewed his struggling. "It's me—Harry. I'm not in prison. Everything is all right, Grandfather."

Charlie came running toward them and he cried out as he came. "Harry! Grandfather said he would bring you back. And he has—he has! Don't hurt him, don't hurt him!"

"Of course we won't hurt him," Harry said. "Grandfather, wake up. You've been in a dream."

Gray Fox ceased his resistance and went limp in his grandson's arms. But only for a moment. In an instant he had recovered and broken away from them, running down the mesa. He was heading for the caves. Harry and Charlie started after him, but he had taken them by surprise and he was well ahead, running as fleetly as any younger man.

Jenny saw him disappear against the shadow of rocky spires, and the echo of his movements came back to them from within the caves.

"Be careful!" Señora Consuelo called to Harry. "It's dangerous down there."

Stones slid and fell as the old man sought

footholds in his escape. Then, suddenly, a sound rose out of the earth that chilled those above—a great rumbling, crashing sound as rock disintegrated and fell in upon itself. The dreadful echoes went on for endless moments, then faded to a whisper, a tiny clatter as the last stones fell. After that there was only silence.

Harry reached the opening first, with Mr. Kingsley right behind him, and their flashlights played upon the black void below. Even the rock of the entrance had caved in so that the opening could be seen in the moonlight.

Señora Consuelo was still holding Jenny and Greg by the arm, but now she let them go and ran toward the men.

"Paul left rope near the entrance," she called to them. "If it hasn't been buried by the rock."

Charlie had reached the two at the cave, and he slipped past them, though his brother snatched at him too late to hold him back.

"I know where the rope is," Charlie called. "Give me your light."

Harry stepped closer to the entrance and threw the beam into the broken cave, and Mr. Kingsley turned his own flashlight upon the opening.

"No one could live through that," Mr. Kingsley said grimly. "He's been buried by tons of rock. I'm afraid it's no use, Charlie."

But Charlie would not listen, and as he found the rope in a crevice above the entrance, a faint, weak sound reached them from below. Jenny found that she was gripping Greg's arm, and that he was as tense as she was.

"He's alive!" Charlie cried. "See! He's been caught on a ledge down there. Not very far down. We're coming, Grandfather!"

Jenny could not see all that happened next, but she could hear. This time Harry pulled his brother from the cave, and he and Mr. Kingsley used the rope Paul Eliot had left behind. It was flung down to Gray Fox and the old man was not too weak to secure it about his waist. As he was pulled up through the jagged opening, there were sounds of more crumbling rock, but though he had been scratched and bruised, he was alive. In a few moments Harry raised him in his arms and carried him to a smooth patch of earth on the mesa. Charlie knelt beside him, speaking to him softly.

"You have succeeded, Grandfather, so now you can rest. Your medicine has brought Harry back."

Harry and Charlie looked at each other with understanding, and the old man seemed to hear their words and rally a little. He raised one hand to show his grandsons that he held the small stone bear of his fetish. Harry too knelt beside him, a quieting hand on his arm. Charlie glanced around and seemed to see those who had climbed the mesa—to see them individually for the first time. His dark gaze rested upon Señora Consuelo.

"I am sorry," he said.

She spoke to him gently. "Perhaps you can tell us now, Charlie?"

Charlie gave her a long, hesitating look.

"It's all right," Harry told his brother. "When I called San Angelo they said that both you and Gray Fox had disappeared, and they knew you were somewhere together. They're waiting for your return. They knew our grandfather would be safe with you. So tell us now how he came here."

Charlie struggled for the right words. "He was upset about the news in the papers and on the radio—about the trial. He didn't think you should go away to help—strangers."

"Other Indians in trouble aren't strangers anymore," Harry said.

Mr. Kingsley spoke softly in agreement. "In our world today no man in trouble can be a stranger."

Charlie went on. "He believed they would put you in prison when the trial ended, Harry. He said they never let an Indian go free. And then he began to think of the old times and he began to believe they would kill you. I saw him when he started away from the pueblo that night, carrying his Shalako things with him. I didn't know at first where he was going. I—I was scared, but it was better to come with him than to let him go alone. There was no time to get help."

"How did you reach the mesa?" Mr. Kingsley asked.

"Once we caught a ride for a little way. But mostly we walked. We haven't forgotten how to walk. We had some food and a little money to buy more on the way. But the food and the money ran out and I had to come down to the ranch. By that time I knew there was trouble with my grandfather. When he began to talk about de Vargas and his attacks upon the pueblos, I knew his mind had gone far back in time."

"So that's why he came to Haunted Mesa," Mr.

Kingsley said. "This is where his people retreated to fortify themselves nearly three hundred years ago. So he came to join them here?"

Charlie bent his head in agreement. Lying on the ground, the old man seemed to hear nothing of what went on above him.

"Sometimes he was in the past and sometimes in today," Charlie continued. "But he never believed he was alone. He looked at me and he thought that his friends and companions had come with him. He believes he was acting with others from San Angelo in coming here. He said they would do everything they could to bring Harry home safely. Only the blessing of the Shalako would do, and he's been performing the ceremonies every day."

"Was it he who took the drum from the museum?" Señora Consuelo asked.

"No." Charlie met her look without wavering. "I'm sorry I had to break the glass. Grandfather said there must be a drum. He sent me to find a drum, and I thought he could make something work for Harry, so I had to try. I didn't steal the drum. It is only borrowed. It will go back now and we will pay for the glass case when I can earn some money."

Jenny found her voice for the first time. "But the kachina dolls, Charlie? It wasn't you in Señora Consuelo's house last night. It couldn't have been."

This was hard for Charlie to tell them about, and he found the words slowly. "My grandfather was in a dream, believing that the people at the ranch were de Vargas' men. When Zuñis hid on the mesa, they sometimes went down on raids to—to get what they needed."

"So he was raiding the Spaniards when he took the kachinas?" Mr. Kingsley said.

"Yes. That's what he believed. He saw the dolls through the window. He thought they should not belong to white men. They should belong to Indian children. So he took one of the dolls. I was with him. I couldn't stop him without making a noise, and I knew we would be arrested if we were caught. So I left a carving—to say I would bring the doll back. But the second time he got away when I didn't know he was gone. He took another doll and he was happy about it. But early this morning, while he slept, I brought both kachinas to the house, and I left my best carving to—to say that I am sorry."

Charlie couldn't have looked more unhappy, and his brother put a hand on his shoulder. "You did what you had to do."

"I'll give the carving back to you," Jenny said softly.

He did not look at her. His eyes were on Mr. Kingsley's face, on Señora Consuelo's, waiting as if for a verdict.

"I'll return the drum," Mr. Kingsley said. "And I'll talk to the ranch director and the director of the museum."

Señora Consuelo nodded her agreement to this plan. "Perhaps Gray Fox has a sickness, Charlie. He is a very old man indeed, and perhaps it would be best for him to go to a hospital."

Harry made a sound of denial, and Charlie looked stricken. He bent over his grandfather, and the old man looked at him dazedly.

"No!" Charlie cried, with more emotion in his

voice than Jenny had ever heard from him. "In a white man's hospital he would die." Then he spoke softly. "It's all over now, Grandfather. Harry has come home. You've brought him home in the blessing of the Shalako. That part is right. But de Vargas' men are gone many years ago. You've been dreaming, Grandfather. It's time to wake up now."

"Yes!" Harry added his own plea. "It's time to wake up. It's time for Gray Fox to go home."

The old man stirred as Charlie shook him gently by the shoulder. After a moment, he rose to his feet with surprising ease. He still wore the deerskin about his waist, and rows of beads glistened in the moonlight on his chest. He had been scratched and bruised by tumbling rock, but he was steady on his feet and he raised his head proudly to face Mr. Kinglsey, peering at him steadily now, as if his head had suddenly cleared.

"You are my friend," he said and held out his hand.

Mr. Kingsley took it. "Of course. I'll take you and Harry back to the pueblo in my car tomorrow. Your people are waiting for you. They knew you would take care of everything."

The old man looked faintly bewildered, but he did not question this place where he found himself, and he allowed Harry to take his arm as they started back toward the trail down the mesa. Charlie picked up the drum with care, and Greg took possession of the blue mask.

Greg appeared a different boy now, touched by the honesty and solemnity of what he had witnessed. When the men started off together with Gray Fox between them, Greg fell into step beside Charlie. The two boys seemed to be talking together, Jenny noted, and was pleased to see them making friends.

Señora Consuelo did not follow the others at once. She stood beside the low ruins of the kiva, lost in her own thoughts, and Jenny did not disturb her. She merely waited. When her friend stirred and looked at her, they both smiled.

"We'd better hurry," Señora Consuelo said. "It will be late by the time we get back to the ranch. But the moon is bright, and we have our flashlights. We'll go carefully."

They walked together after the others, and silence lay gently upon them. There was no need to talk. A strange experience had been shared and it was necessary to think about it quietly.

Once Jenny thought about Carol, who would be sound asleep by the time they got back. She didn't really have to be like Carol. She didn't even *want* to be like her anymore. And she didn't ever need to envy her again. Somehow she had grown up a little in these few days, so that everything she looked at was changed a little. If she ever wanted to be like anyone, it would be Consuelo Eliot she would choose. But mostly she would be very busy finding out how to be herself, and there would be no time left over for being the tail of anyone else's kite.

"Could you drive me to San Angelo Pueblo sometime?" she asked Señora Consuelo. "I'd like to see where Gray Fox lives. And I want to give that carving back to Charlie. I didn't have a chance to tell him how beautiful I think it is."

Señora Consuelo's smile was luminous in the pale

light. "I'll be happy to take you there, Jenny," she promised, and they started down the trail together.

Above them, Haunted Mesa dreamed in the moonlight. No one would ever again go down into the chimney of the caves, but the spirit of the mountain had been generous tonight. Who was to know what misty memories stirred on the mesa? Who was to hear the faint, far sound of a ghostly drum?

Author's Note

I want to thank the staff of Ghost Ranch, which is located near Abiquiu, New Mexico, for their kindness and courtesy when I visited the ranch. The Haunted Mesa Ranch of this story is an entirely fictional version of the beautiful Ghost Ranch area. I have taken geographical liberties in using Zuñi Indians in this particular region. There is no San Angelo Pueblo, and the Zuñis are actually farther away near Gallup. Their art and ceremonies, however, are real, and so is my treatment of Indian problems today. There were probably few Spanish settlers in this region originally, though Black Mesa, to the south, was used as a refuge, as is the mesa in my story.

About the Author

Phyllis A. Whitney was born of American parents in Yokohama, Japan, where her father was in business. Later the family lived in the Philippines and China. After her father's death, she and her mother returned to the States, which she saw for the first time at age fifteen. In this country she has lived in Berkeley, San Antonio, and Chicago, and presently resides on Long Island, New York.

Phyllis Whitney has been writing since the age of fifteen, first short stories and then her first book in 1941. To date she has published over fifty novels, many of which are for young people. Her books have been translated into seventeen languages, with millions of copies in paperback and hardcover in more than 200 editions. In recent years she has published some eighteen adult suspense novels. Her own daughter loved to read her books when she was growing up, and now enjoys the adult novels. Phyllis Whitney's three grandchildren are presently following in their mother's footsteps.

The author has spent much time in travel, with many of her books set in areas she has visited or lived in. She works six days a week at her writing, usually mornings from 8 to 11; after time out in midday, she returns to writing until 4:30 or 5.

She has won a number of awards for her books for young people, twice receiving the "Edgar" Award of the Mystery Writers of America. She spent a year with the Chicago Public Library and has been Children's Book Editor for both *The Chicago Sun* and *The Philadelphia Inquirer*. She was instructor in Juvenile Fiction Writing at Northwestern University and taught for eleven years at New York University. Presently all her time is given to writing, with usually two books a year, one for young people and one for adults.